THE HOOKUP HOAX

HEATHER THURMEIER

Entangled Publishing, LLC
2614 South Timberline Road
Suite 109
Fort Collins, CO 80525
Visit our website at www.entangledpublishing.com.

Lovestruck is an imprint of Entangled Publishing, LLC.

Edited by Alethea Spiridon Hopson
Cover design by Heather Howland
Photography by iStock

Manufactured in the United States of America

First Edition May 2015

To my girls,
I hope one day—when you're both much, much older—you can read my books and not be embarrassed that your mum wrote the steamy scenes.

To Mike,
Thank you for making my real life even better than a romance novel.

Chapter One

Sawyer Sterling sipped his ice-cold cola and wished it wasn't too early to add a splash of rum to the glass. As CEO of Sterling Enterprises, a marketing company in New York City, he had to be clearheaded and focused at all times if he wanted his business to be successful. And he did, but it was getting more and more challenging every year.

At the moment he couldn't focus on anything. Not the fact they were currently short-staffed because of an unexpected medical leave, or the fact that this quarter was the worst he'd seen in his years as CEO. And he definitely couldn't focus on the meeting with a prospective client he had to plan for—a client with a deal big enough to turn the numbers around for the whole year.

Today his focus was shot to hell because he couldn't stop thinking about the news he'd gotten last night, at Sunday dinner with his family.

"What's wrong with you?" Aidan asked. "That waitress

with the sweet ass walked by our table again, and again you failed to notice. Something happen at the office this morning? Or did that girl in the silver dress ride you so hard on Friday night that you're still recovering?"

It wasn't unusual for him to go home with a girl on his arm, though he didn't make it a weekly event. But every now and then, one would catch his eye, sexual chemistry would spark, and panties would fly off, as if by magic.

When the job got hard, his dick seemed to stiffen up, too, and there was only one cure for that. Well, two really. But a solo tug in the shower was the equivalent of rubbing your temples to cure a migraine, when what you really needed was a couple of extra-strength painkillers.

"Work is the same." His grandfather's company had been successful once upon a time. His father had taken over when Gramps was getting ready to retire, and he'd made it even bigger in the field. Then his parents died, and Sterling Enterprises had been left in the hands of an interim CEO until Sawyer's eighteenth birthday. When he'd finally taken over, he'd been left with nothing more than memories of his father's legacy, the shell of what had once been a thriving business, and the overwhelming fear that he'd never measure up, no matter how hard he tried. Nothing new there. "It's the family situation that's suddenly gotten out of control."

His best friend's brow creased. "You haven't gotten some girl knocked up, have you?"

"God no." Sawyer shuddered at the thought. He was always safe. He didn't do serious relationships, and a baby definitely made a situation serious. "It's nothing like that."

Aidan relaxed back into his seat. "So what is it then?"

Sawyer looked at his drink and trailed his fingers through

the condensation on the outside of the glass. It reminded him of the water droplets rolling off Rosemary's shoulders as she climbed out of the lake last summer. At least he thought that was her name. Could have been Rosaline. Roseanne? Regardless, watching water running down her tight body had been a pretty damned fantastic way to spend a day with one of the locals. "You know my grandparents' place?"

Aidan nodded, as expected. His friend couldn't forget the place where Sawyer had lived for so long, anymore than he could. "What about it?"

"They've decided to move back into the city, where they'll have more access to everything."

"That's great. Why do you look like that's a death sentence?"

"They think the place should go to someone who will keep it in the family, pass it down through the generations like they're doing. There's only me and my cousin Tyler. I can't help but feel like they're forcing my hand. I mean, how can I compete with the guy who has a pregnant wife?"

Growing up, his grandparents' cabin in the Catskills was the one place he really connected with his dad...the one place where his father wasn't too busy with work to spend time with him. Later, after his parents died, the cabin had gone from summer vacation spot to permanent residence in the blink of an eye, when he'd moved in with his grandparents full-time. The cabin had become home. Now they were passing it down. The thought that it could go to someone other than himself, especially his obnoxious cousin, made his stomach twist into a tight knot.

The one place he loved and hated most in the world—the source of his best family memories, and the site of the boating accident that took his parents' lives.

"Your grandparents can't really expect you to settle down just because they want to leave the cabin to someone with a family, can they?"

"You do remember my grandparents, right? Overbearing. Protective. Meddling." They were also sweet, loving, and kind, but it was hard to remember that at the moment. Not to mention, they were the ones who'd stood by him, taken him in, given him a place to live after his parents died.

Aidan laughed. "How can I forget? Gran called me last week to grill me on why I haven't been out to see them in months. As if I haven't spent enough Sunday dinners at their place since middle school. And if I don't show my face before their big birthday party, I'm not to show my face at all. Disowned." He laughed again. "It's like she's forgotten my last name is Morgan, not Sterling. You can't disown something you didn't own in the first place."

"You can't be friends with me this long and not be considered part of the family. The sooner you realize you've officially been adopted by Gran, the better off you'll be."

Aidan's cell vibrated with a new text message. He typed a response as the waitress delivered his pizza, and a burger for Sawyer. "Can I order a clubhouse sandwich with fries and a side of gravy as well?" he asked her.

The waitress nodded and walked away. Aidan was right. She did have a fabulous ass.

"Pizza isn't enough? Did you pick up a tape worm or something?" Sawyer asked, eyeing his friend and his abnormally huge appetite.

"No. It's for Olivia. She's crashing on my couch. I told her she could join us for a quick bite since I don't have any food in the house. I hope you don't mind. I'm sure she'll just eat and leave."

Memories of childhood flooded his thoughts. He couldn't count the number of hours he'd spent running around outside on warm summer nights with Aidan and Olivia. It hadn't mattered that that she was Aidan's little sister by two years. She'd kept up with them—playing ball, riding bikes, and skinning her knees while climbing trees right along with them. Someone could've mistaken her for just another boy if it hadn't been for her long, braided pigtails. The three of them had been almost inseparable until…

He shook his head, not wanting to think about his parents' accident again. It had happened. It was in the past. So was Olivia and Aidan's parents' divorce, which had happened shortly afterward. Olivia had gone to live with her mom, and Aidan had stayed in New York with his dad. All three kids hit a rough patch in life at the same time—exactly why real relationships were bad news for everyone.

"I didn't know she was in town. I thought she was still backpacking. How long is she crashing with you before she heads home to California?"

Aidan shrugged. "Forever, at this point. She's decided to try the East Coast lifestyle for a while. I guess she can stay as long as she needs to, to get back on her feet."

"It's not easy starting from scratch in this city. It's good you're letting her crash with you." Sawyer grinned and picked up his burger. "I'm sure the girl you try to bring home next weekend won't mind finding your sister on the couch."

"Not much I can do about it," Aidan said. "So what about you? What are you going to do about your grandparents' place?"

Sawyer took a bite of his burger and chewed thoughtfully. "They never actually said I had to get married, thank God, but being able to pass it down in the future is definitely their biggest concern. Being single shouldn't make me deserve it less. Hell, it's been my home for years. I'll take good care of it."

Marriage and babies—long-term relationships in general—were not something he was interested in, now or ever. Not that he was against commitment for other people, just for himself. Marriages were great. Families were great—until he was the orphaned kid, left behind to be raised by his grandparents. Then the thought of marriage and family sucked. There was no way he'd risk having a wife or family while knowing he could die at any moment, leaving behind a wake of sadness and loneliness. It was easier not to get into the situation to begin with. Bachelorhood for life, and no collateral damage.

Sawyer pushed his plate aside, his appetite gone. "I can't let it go to Tyler. He doesn't even like it out there."

After a long silence, Aidan spoke. "If all they want is to see you in a relationship, why not let them?"

Sawyer shook his head. "I don't do relationships, you know that." He'd mistakenly thought he could handle one a few years ago, only to have it end in a messy break-up. Tammy had wanted to be put first, like any girlfriend would, but he'd been focused only on living up to his father's legacy, and making the business successful once again, not on nurturing a romance.

"You don't do *real* relationships," his friend said, "but what if you find someone to play your girlfriend for a little while? Someone you could show off to the family? They'd get what they want, and hopefully after their birthday party, you'll get what you want, too—the cabin. Pretend to break up a month later and no one will be the wiser."

He might not want a real girlfriend, but he could deal with a fake girlfriend if it meant the cabin would be his in three months.

He nodded. "Okay, but what kind of woman would sign up for this, knowing they'd be tossing away three months of their life for nothing?"

"There must be someone. Not every woman wants long-term."

Sawyer laughed. "Really? When was the last time you met a girl who *didn't* want forever?"

"Good point," Aiden admitted. "What about that girl Sasha you went out with last month?"

The girls he "dated" were usually eager to move from the hookup part to the girlfriend stage. With any of them, a fake relationship might become too real on their end. He wanted to keep his home, but he didn't want to hurt anyone along the way. He still felt a tiny twinge of remorse when he thought about how much he'd hurt Tammy. That was another mistake he didn't want to repeat in the future. "Nope. No ex-hookups."

"Okay. What about your receptionist?" Aidan asked as the waitress set down the clubhouse sandwich at the empty spot at the table.

"Definitely not." Sawyer sighed. "She came into work with an engagement ring on her finger a few weeks ago, and there's no one else at work I'd consider. Besides, it has to be someone my family will believe I would suddenly date."

Aidan waved toward the front door, past Sawyer's

shoulder. "Olivia's here."

Sawyer's mouth dropped open. This wasn't the kid he knew from years ago. Gone was her boyishly rectangular frame and dirt-stained cheeks, replaced by flowing curves and tantalizingly tanned flesh. She wasn't a kid anymore.

Olivia was a woman.

A fucking sexy one, too.

As Olivia plunked herself at her brother's side, Sawyer couldn't pull his gaze away. While he still recognized hints of the kid she used to be, he liked the ways she'd changed. Her lips were fuller now and softly coated in color, exactly the kind of lips he loved to kiss. Long ago the thought of kissing her had been disgusting, but now…he could almost imagine the warmth of her plump lips as his tongue flicked across them.

"Hi," she said with a quick, unsure smile, meeting his gaze for merely a second then turning her attention to her brother. "Thanks for ordering. I'm starving."

She grabbed a stacked triangle of sandwich and dipped it into the bowl of gravy before sinking her teeth into it. The sigh that escaped her mouth was one of pure pleasure, and her eyelids fluttered shut.

Sawyer swallowed hard. That sound…it was enough to make his balls tighten.

Aidan cleared his throat and Sawyer met his friend's eyes. The expression staring back at him was angry and protective. "You're welcome. I'm happy to keep my *little sis* fed while she's staying with me."

There was no doubt in Sawyer's mind why he'd emphasized certain words. Message received. Little sis was off-limits. But that shouldn't mean he couldn't look.

"So," he said, hoping to sound cheerful and aloof, "are you having trouble finding an apartment? I can't imagine the couch is very comfortable."

"She can't move out until she has a paycheck, and she can't earn a paycheck if she can't find a job."

"No one will give you a job?" Sawyer asked. "That doesn't seem right."

Olivia shrugged. "Seems 'kiwi picker in New Zealand' doesn't earn much respect on a resume these days. I mean, I worked hard to earn my pay. It's not like I was sitting around on a beach for years working on my tan."

Her skin was a warm caramel, but the neckline of her shirt had slipped off her shoulder while she ate, revealing a tan line that proved just how milky white her skin normally was. Maybe she wasn't a professional beach bum, but she'd definitely seen her fair share of sunshine recently, more than they'd had here in New York City in the last few months. As his gaze followed the tan line where it disappeared beneath her shirt, he found himself wondering how sun-kissed the rest of her body was. Surf-loving New Zealanders liked bikinis, didn't they? When in Rome, as they say…

Forcing his thoughts on to safer topics, he swallowed his last bite of burger before speaking again. "Didn't you do any other work while you backpacked around the world? Surely something you did must be good enough for a resume."

"Would you hire a kiwi picker, coffee server, or farm hand who hadn't been in the country for the last five years?"

Sawyer's thoughts filled with images of Olivia on the top of a ladder with her head stuck in a kiwi plant. He could imagine the kid he knew back in middle school doing something like that, but this put-together-without-being-high-maintenance woman in front of him? No way. She definitely looked more suited for an office job somewhere instead of out in a field getting dirty.

Huh.

Crashing on a couch. In need of an apartment and a job.

Maybe...

Olivia was Aidan's little sister.

His smirk grew into a grin. She glanced up from her plate, flinching suddenly when she found him eyeing her. He knew he should look away, but couldn't. Olivia was safe. She was protected by the Bro Code. Little sisters of buddies were always off-limits, as Aidan had already made perfectly clear. There was no way Sawyer would be tempted to get involved with her in any way, when doing so would jeopardize his friendship.

"Why are you grinning like a guy who knows two weeks in advance which team would win the Super Bowl?" Aidan asked.

Sawyer leaned forward, his elbows resting on the table, giving all his attention to Olivia and ignoring his friend. "I'll hire you."

"You will?" she asked. "But you don't even know my qualifications."

"What was your major?"

"I graduated with a BA in Business."

"Perfect. We have an administrative assistant position that's available because Bethany had to take a medical leave."

"That's great," Olivia said, enthusiastically. "Not for Bethany, of course, but for me. I can fill in until she's well enough to return to work."

"Are you sure you want to do that? You don't need to feel obligated to hire her because of our friendship," Aidan said.

"Shut up," Olivia whispered, nudging her brother in the side. "I need a job."

"Yeah, but you'd have to work with *him*."

"What's wrong with that?" she asked, still whispering.

Sawyer cleared his throat as a subtle hint that while they could obviously see him, he could also hear them. When they turned his way, he wove his fingers together as if he was about to pray. Maybe he should, if it meant this new plan had a hope of working. "On one condition."

Aidan grimaced. "What's that exactly? And before you answer, remember she's my sister and I will hurt you." Sawyer didn't know why, exactly, but ever since Olivia had graduated college and gone off to travel, Aidan had been especially protective of her.

"I can speak for myself. What's your condition?" she asked, before taking another bite of her sandwich and shoving in a few fries for good measure. The girl could eat.

"I'll hire you. I'll even offer you my guest room, rent free. All you have to do is agree to be my girlfriend for a while."

Olivia choked and reached for her water. After taking a good, long chug, she spoke. "I would be your girlfriend, why, exactly?"

"It wouldn't be real," Sawyer said. "You'd only have to pretend."

"No way." Aidan sat back in his chair, his arms folded across his chest. The waitress collected his empty dish and asked if they needed anything else. "The bill. We're done here."

He knew, by the look on Aidan's face, he meant they were done with more than the meal. But Sawyer wasn't done. He always got what he wanted, and right now he wanted Olivia. She was the perfect choice.

He knew having Olivia around had to be cramping his friend's style. Aidan liked to bring girls back to his place, and he couldn't do that with her on the couch. "Think about it. She'll be out of your hair. All she has to do is pretend to be my girlfriend at a few family functions and dinners for the next few months. Easy."

"I don't like the thought of you and Olivia...together," Aidan practically growled. All his brotherly protectiveness was aimed squarely at Sawyer, as if he would hurt her on purpose, which he never would. Although, he hadn't meant to hurt Tammy either, and both men knew how that turned out.

"We won't be together. Not really, anyway."

A blob of gravy dripped onto Olivia's shirt and her frown increased as she tried to wipe it away. Sawyer was momentarily mesmerized by the jiggle of her breasts as she dabbed at the stain with a napkin.

Aidan coughed, and Sawyer's gaze darted back to his friend, his mind suddenly in the conversation again. "This was your idea in the first place, Aidan. I can't even think about your little sister in the way I think of other women. That would be...weird."

Except for right now, with her jiggling breasts. And that moment earlier when she was eating. And her plump, kissable lips... I'll stop all that, starting now.

"Still sitting here," she said, waving her hand as if trying to get their attention. She had his attention. She had since the moment she walked in the door, but her good looks wouldn't change the fact that she was off-limits and therefore the safest bet he could make. Neither one of them would risk getting involved in a relationship, or even a fling, when they had big brother Aidan playing chaperone between them.

Sawyer focused on Aidan. He had to get his friend on board or there was no hope of this working. He needed a plan, quick. "If she agrees, then give us your blessing and trust me."

"I can't imagine why she'd ever agree to this," he grumbled.

"I can." Sawyer smiled, this time turning to Olivia. "You need an apartment, with an actual room and a bed of your own to sleep in, and you need a job that pays real money and provides you with a reference for your resume. I need you to be my girlfriend—*fake* girlfriend—starting now, until my grandparents celebrate their birthdays."

There was a long pause.

"I'm still confused," she said around a bite of sandwich.

"My grandparents are old grumps and don't want to give their cabin to someone who can't pass it down to future generations, and I need to prove to them I am that someone. Therefore, I need a girlfriend. *Fake* girlfriend. Temporarily."

"You don't have a real girlfriend to date?" She eyed him suspiciously. Her gaze raking across his body felt unusually critical, and his defenses rose.

"Nope. I don't do long-term relationships, but that's beside the point. Listen, I know it's unusual, but I really need your help. It's win-win. You'll save up money and earn job experience, and I'll get the cabin. Once that happens, we'll both go our separate ways, no harm, no foul, and both better off. So what do you say? You can't possibly enjoy living with Aidan. I could tell you all kinds of stories I've heard about things he's done on that couch. *Who* he's done on that couch."

"Dude!" Aidan said, scrunching up his face in disgust. "She probably still thinks I'm a virgin."

"Stop!" Olivia demanded. "Don't say anything else. And no one thinks you're a virgin anymore, Aidan. I saw the econo-sized box of condoms in the bathroom cabinet." She met Sawyer's gaze. "I'll do it, but I have one condition of my own. You promise to never, *ever* tell me sex stories about my brother."

Sawyer laughed, the thrill of success shooting through him like endorphins. It was the same feeling he got every time he signed a new client at work. "Absolutely."

Aidan pointed at his sister then at Sawyer and then drew his finger across his own neck in a straight line. Sawyer got the message. Mess with sister, death by brother.

The sister in question rolled her eyes. "Real subtle, overprotective brother."

He scrawled his address on a mostly clean napkin and handed it across the table. Their hands touched as she took it and, for a moment, he was hesitant to let go. Her fingers tingled in his palm. Surely it was those endorphins still coursing through his system. "Here's my address. You can come by the apartment whenever. You must be ready for a good night's sleep in a real bed by now."

"Okay. Tonight at eight?"

Sawyer held her gaze, ignoring her brother, while feeling smug that his quick thinking had paid off. "Eight works."

Aidan scowled. "If you hurt my little sister, I'll chop off

your balls, mince them, fry them, wrap them in tortillas, then invite you over for tacos. Got it?"

Olivia burst out laughing. "Oh my God, so much for trying to be subtle."

Sawyer shook his head and got up from the table. "Loud and clear. And visually descriptive."

Chapter Two

Olivia knocked on the door to Sawyer's apartment and looped her hands around the straps of her backpack. If there was one skill she'd mastered during her years of traveling, it was packing light and fast. Anywhere, anytime, she was ready to go. It was also the biggest reason she'd come back to the States. Seeing the world, being in new places, and different cultures was unlike any other experience. But traveling, on her own for the most part, had taken its toll. It had been wonderful, amazing, life changing…and lonely.

She was ready to settle down. Plant roots. Make a home base. A place she could call hers. More than anything, she wanted stability and someone to share it with.

Her thumb instinctively rubbed against the third finger of her left hand. It had been five years since she'd almost had the life she wanted. Five years since Sam said his proposal was a mistake and had left her, days before their wedding. But that life was long gone, along with the weight of the ring on her finger, leaving behind nothing but untouched skin and a once-broken, but now-mended, heart.

New York was supposed to be her fresh start, far from the sunny west coast and the pain she'd left behind when she'd decided to travel after graduating from college, instead of going straight into a job. She thought it would be easy to come to a new city, find a job, and get a little apartment. Turned out no one wanted to hire someone who didn't stay in one place longer than a season. No one wanted to give her a chance to prove she hadn't forgotten everything she'd learned earning her business degree.

So here she was, outside Sawyer's door. Her door. Their door.

She still couldn't believe she'd agreed to this arrangement.

The lock slipped inside the door, and she said a quick, silent prayer that she hadn't made a huge mistake. What did she even know about Sawyer anymore, after all these years? And yet she'd agreed to live with him, date him?

Fake date, but still… What was I thinking?

She straightened her shoulders and tried to look confident, yet casual. *I was thinking I need a job and money.* This was her only option right now.

As the door opened, Olivia plastered a large, hopefully friendly smile on her face, but as Sawyer's large frame filled the doorway, the corners of her lips slowly drooped. Standing before her was not the tall, somewhat lanky, pre-adolescent boy she remembered. He'd always been athletic, but never really what you'd call muscular. That boy was gone, replaced by a man.

A man who looked as if he could be an underwear model. Her gaze darted downward to the area in question, wondering if he'd be a boxer or brief man in that commercial.

Had he looked like this at the restaurant, too?

Surely he hadn't. Of course, she'd woken up late and had barely made it to lunch, and she'd been distracted by her brother being there. But damn. Sawyer looked way hotter now than he had when she'd agreed to this arrangement. Or maybe it was the casual jeans and T-shirt he wore now, instead of the business suit he'd worn earlier, that caught her attention. The form-fitting T showed off the lines and contours of his muscles, while the green material made his blue eyes almost sparkle.

"Olivia." He smiled in a way that lit up his whole face and pulled her in for a hug. "I can't get over how much older you look."

"Thanks, I think," she said, attempting to sound aloof while her heart pounded. If this was equivalent to a business deal, then why the hell was she so nervous all of a sudden? Why did it feel so good to have his chest pressed against hers in what should be an innocent hug?

Olivia glanced up as she walked past him into the apartment. He had to be almost a full foot taller than her. His eyes were still the pools of turquoise she remembered. A hint of stubble dusted a chiseled jaw, giving away the late hour of the day. She'd tried to make it to his apartment by eight as planned, but Aidan had insisted on giving her "the talk" about Sawyer being a player and how to beat him off with a stick if necessary.

She wouldn't need to.

What Sawyer looked like now was of little interest to her. She didn't want to get involved with a guy who was proud to be a bachelor for life. She wanted someone to settle down and build a life with. And that someone would never be Sawyer Sterling, even if they were playing house temporarily.

Being off the dating market for a few months might be a long time to some girls, but Olivia needed this time to put her own life first, and then, once she was ready, she'd worry about finding a good guy. Until then, Sawyer was a safe bet to pretend "date," since there was no risk of falling in love with him to get in the way of her other plans. As an added bonus, her fake relationship with him would keep her at an arm's length from anyone else who could possibly become a distraction before she was ready to date for real.

"I don't think that came out right." He grinned sheepishly.

When he smiled, a little dimple puckered in his cheek. Something about dimples made a man look so innocent and unassuming, even as they plotted to tear the clothes from her body to ravish her. Or at least that's what they did in her daydreams. Dimples, combined with that raised eyebrow thing he'd apparently mastered and was doing right now... *wow*.

"Not older as in old. Just you grew up. Matured." He ran his fingers through his hair while his gaze skimmed her top to bottom and back, leaving a wake of heat behind.

Did he just check me out? No. Not likely. It was the dimple effect causing her brain and body to malfunction, nothing more.

"It has been a while, hasn't it?"

"Fifteen years, I think. Crazy. I still remember when you fell and skinned your knee that time we went riding on the bike trails through Sherwood Park. Or that time you insisted your parents said it was okay for you to use the waffle iron, and then you almost set the kitchen on fire. I was turned off waffles for years."

"One time I leave the plastic spatula touching the waffle maker, and no one forgets, but the other millions of times I made perfect waffles, no one remembers." She laughed at the memories of happier times before everything in their worlds changed. Not long after that, Sawyer's parents had their accident, and then her parents decided to suddenly call it quits, moving her to California while Aidan stayed in New York.

Just another reason she'd come back here. This time, she wasn't leaving.

"I'm sure you learned how to make delicious waffles. Eventually."

"People beg for a taste of my waffles." She raised an eyebrow teasingly.

"I bet they do." His eyes glimmered mischievously, like she'd seen so many times when he'd plotted something devious with her brother. "Did you bring one this time? I wouldn't mind a taste."

His words lingered between them as her pulse suddenly raced.

He straightened and glanced around as if he'd been caught looking at a dirty magazine in church.

That wasn't an innuendo… was it? Surely it was her imagination, and his discomfort was from something else. She laughed off his comment. "No room in my backpack for a waffle iron, I'm afraid. I've learned to live with less in my *old* age."

"I gather you didn't have any trouble finding the apartment." As he folded his arms across his chest, she couldn't help but notice how tightly his fitted T-shirt clung to his muscular form.

"I found you hot. Here. *Fine!* I found your apartment fine." Apparently her tongue and brain were both on the fritz.

His lips turned up slightly, as if he were trying to hide a grin. She attempted to channel the inner calm she'd learned to tap into during meditation in Thailand. She'd never been the kind of girl who got flustered around a guy before, and she sure as hell wasn't about to start now.

"I made you an apartment key this afternoon." He placed it in her outstretched hand, his fingers gliding across her palm like a breeze on the surface of a lake. The sensation sent a tremble rippling through her. She gripped the key tightly, steadying her hand and her nerves.

He wasn't allowed to have this effect on her. He was safe, temporary, and unsuitable for her future. She repeated the words in her head, hoping they'd stick.

"Let me take this for you. It looks heavy." Sawyer lifted the backpack from her shoulders.

"I carried that around the world. I'm sure I could have managed to get it to the guest room too."

"The ability to go anywhere you wanted with only what you could carry on your back, to not be tied down to one place, that must have been amazingly…freeing." His voice held such a tone of longing as he peered at her backpack. But why would he long for that life? He had so much here— his family, his friends, a successful company, and a gorgeous apartment.

"It was nice. For a while."

He led her down the hall to her new room. It was larger

than any space she'd been able to call her own in almost ten years, between college dorms and traveling. The queen-sized bed looked inviting, with a blanket fluffy enough to swallow her whole. A quick glance into the open closet and she knew she'd never be able to fill even a quarter of it with her meager belongings.

"I hope this is enough space for you. Whenever you're ready to move in the rest of your things, let me know. I'd be happy to help."

She patted her backpack. "This is everything."

"So you're officially all moved in then." The smile fell from his face as if he'd said something offensive by accident. His brow furrowed and his gaze darted to the hallway before he cleared his throat and pulled open another door. "The bathroom is through here."

She peeked inside. Clean. Not like some of the hostels she'd stayed in. Definitely not at all what she expected a bachelor's bathroom to look like. There was a full bathtub she couldn't wait to soak in, a steam shower, and a large double vanity—easily enough space for both of them.

"Towels?" she asked, pointing at another door. If he didn't have any extras, she'd have to run out and buy some for herself. The one she'd carried with her traveling had been tossed the second she'd stepped on home soil, and she'd been using the ones her brother had on hand.

"Those are in the hall closet. You can help yourself." He walked through the space and opened the door in question. "It's a second entrance from my room. Hopefully that won't be a problem. Both doors lock, and we'll figure out some sort of schedule."

"I'm sure it'll be fine," she said, forcing her voice to

sound aloof. She figured sharing a bathroom was likely, but sharing a bathroom that connected to both bedrooms? That was a little too cozy for her comfort.

"I'll leave you to get settled in. If you're hungry or thirsty or anything, the kitchen is stocked. If you need help finding something, just ask. Otherwise I'll assume you'll use this apartment as if it were your own, because it is, sort of. For now at least."

Once Sawyer closed his door to the bathroom, she closed hers as well, then her bedroom door leading to the hall. When she was totally enclosed in her new space, she flopped back onto her bed and puffed out her breath, feeling as if she'd been holding it since she'd knocked on the door.

Was this room really hers? All of this space to herself, for three months, seemed too good to be true. She had to share the rest of the apartment with Sawyer—a task she'd thought would be easy. But now, after seeing him again, she wasn't so sure. Most likely she was experiencing the same shock any-one would at seeing someone from her past again after so long. There'd been a few moments when she'd caught Saw-yer looking at her, studying her as if he was shocked by what he saw too. Surely, the way her heart pounded in her chest was a symptom of their reunion and nothing more.

She could not, would not, feel anything for Sawyer. He was her brother's best friend, her dating safety net while she got settled into her new life, and her boss. And after everything that happened with Sam, she'd sworn off playboy bachelor-types. She hadn't met a woman yet who could reform a man like that, herself included, and she certainly would never let herself make that mistake twice.

No, nada, nope. Gorgeous hunk of man-candy or not, he

was off-limits.

Olivia worked steadily until she was settled into her new room. The task took barely an hour, with her meager belongings. When she'd woken this morning on Aidan's couch, she hadn't had a single drawer to put her things in, now she had an entire room. Somehow her day had taken an unexpected twist, and here she was sharing an apartment and on the cusp of starting a new job. Things were finally getting on track.

Her new bed called to her. She climbed into the cozy blankets and curled up with her novel.

She startled awake as the book flopped onto her face, smacking the bridge of her nose.

Rolling over, she set it on the nightstand then closed her eyes, trying to fall back into blissful dreamland, but her dry throat demanded she find water. Smoothing down her nightshirt, she wished it were a couple of inches longer. Of course, she could always pull on yoga pants and a sweater, but her trip to the kitchen would be quick.

Peeking out into the hallway, Olivia listened for Sawyer. They might be roomies now, and had known each other for years, technically, but that didn't mean she was comfortable wandering around nearly naked in front of him. The way he'd looked at her tonight, fully clothed, had been enough to send her heartbeat drumming in her ears.

Light seeped from under his bedroom door. It was earlier than she'd expected him to call it a night, but he was a top dog at Sterling Enterprises and maybe he was one of those executives who got up at the crack of dawn to workout, so he went to bed earlier than most. That would explain the muscles.

She crept down the hallway, curious about the rest of the apartment. Sawyer hadn't given her the full tour of his place — *their* place — earlier, but she didn't mind. She'd been too caught off guard by his good looks, his filled out and grown up body, and the sexy glint in his eyes when he'd welcomed her to pay attention to apartment details.

Stop, she scolded herself. *Friend zone only. No trespassing, remember?*

Past a tastefully appointed living room, which was far too put together to belong in a bachelor's apartment, she spotted bright lights reflecting off a stainless steel fridge. She trailed her hand along the back of the couch as she walked by, stopping to stroke the throw blanket draped across the cushions. She couldn't imagine a guy like Sawyer under a blanket like this in the evening, watching TV. The thought of Sawyer's bare chest was enough to make her mouth go dry. Well, drier than it already was.

Most likely the blanket had been put there just for looks. Not for long. She could already picture herself snuggled into the big armchair in the corner, bundled up in the soft, knitted throw, reading.

Walking through the doorway, Olivia froze at the sight of Sawyer leaning against the counter, head tilted back while he chugged orange juice directly out of the container. A dribble of liquid escaped the side of his mouth and rolled down his neck.

Olivia swallowed, salivating as if she'd been starving a week and had just been granted access to a Vegas-style buffet. She inhaled through her teeth, her breath skipping into her lungs.

He startled, lowering the jug of juice. The liquid sloshed

as he shook it. "Want some?" he asked, holding it out toward her.

"No thanks. I need a glass of water."

He grinned then drained the rest of the container before tossing it into the recycling bin. "I guess I should start using a glass, huh? It's been a while since I've had a roommate."

"Probably wouldn't hurt, although you're safe with orange juice since I don't like it." Or at least she didn't like it last time she'd had it. Having just watched it drip down his body, she wasn't so sure she felt that way anymore.

"Glasses are in the cabinet to the right of the sink, on the middle shelf. Or if you prefer, there's bottled water in the refrigerator." He spoke as if he wasn't uncomfortable sharing his space.

She wished she could say the same. Eventually, she hoped to feel comfortable in this apartment, but she currently felt like a visitor spending the night. It was awkward to wander around as if she had a right to be there, like it was home.

"I'll grab a glass. I prefer not to throw out plastic bottles if possible. I usually have a reusable one with me, but I must have left it at Aidan's. I'll stop by his place tomorrow to pick it up."

"You're not one of those crazy environmentalists, are you? You're not going to throw red paint on my leather coat or anything?" He eyed her, clearly suspicious.

Olivia rolled her eyes, mildly annoyed that he'd be more concerned about the safety of his jacket than the damage to the earth everyone contributed to. "Aside from ruining clothing and overstepping a few personal boundaries, there's nothing wrong with people who believe in protecting our environment." She sighed, trying to let her irritation subside. Just because she cared, didn't mean she would force other people to care as well. "But no, I'm not one of them, so your leather products are safe."

Of course, people like Sawyer could make an effort and at least switch to reusable bottles and bags. She shrugged while images from the last five years flashed through her mind. "I've seen a lot in my travels and, as a whole, our culture is wasteful. I figure if I'm a little more conscientious, it can't hurt."

Far from a saint herself, she wasn't about to preach to Sawyer or anyone else about how they should live their lives, or what products they should consume or use. But when it came down to it, she tried to make choices she felt good about. After seeing how bad it was in other parts of the world, she felt privileged to be able to grab clean water straight out of the tap.

Turning her back to Sawyer, she opened the cabinet and reached up to the middle shelf. She never really thought of herself as short until she had to perch on the balls of her feet to reach something, feeling the stretch through her entire body, like a yoga instructor. Just as her hand circled the glass, a cool breeze blew across her right butt cheek.

Her exposed right butt cheek.

Why did I wear a thong today? Couldn't I take two seconds to put on pants?

Quickly, she lowered her arm. As she did, the soft cotton of her nightshirt slid back over her rear, covering her. She swallowed hard.

Did he see? Please be looking anywhere else...

She turned, gripping her newly acquired glass.

His gaze hit her right around the tops of her thighs then

slowly traveled up the length of her body before settling on her eyes. Every nerve ending came to life under his scrutiny. His jaw muscle bulged as if he was clenching his teeth.

Oh, he saw. Everything.

"I…" she said, then closed her eyes while trying to think of something appropriate to say. *Sorry I just flashed you my ass? Thongs, huh? Can't depend on them for coverage!*

She bit her lower lip and forced her eyes open. She was a big girl. Surely she could face a minor awkward moment head on. Olivia met his gaze while pulling a quivering breath into her tight lungs.

"I…"

"I'm going to bed," he said quickly, holding her gaze. His eyes sparkled in the bright kitchen lights, like the sun reflecting off the ocean. "I have an early meeting. Tomorrow, I'll get everything sorted out for your new job and bring home any paperwork you need to fill out. You can start first thing next week, okay?" He stared at her for a moment before pushing off the counter and walking out of the room with what she thought was a sigh.

Could've been a quiet groan.

"Thank you," she called weakly after him, thrilled for the change in topic, and for his chivalrous behavior concerning her wardrobe malfunction… until she realized that not only had her *platonic*, fake-boyfriend and roommate just seen her naked ass cheek—so had her new boss.

Chapter Three

Sawyer stopped the car and turned off the ignition in front of the cabin that had been his home during his middle school and high school years. A quiver of emotion bloomed to life in his chest, as it did every time he came to visit. When he'd lived there growing up, he'd been numbed to the sensation, but after living in the city for years, coming back home to the cabin was always a mix of sadness and happiness at the memories of his parents and the time spent with his grandparents.

The cabin was a sprawling ranch-style home. Along the front façade, rows of windows looked out over the gently sloped lawn, dotted with trees. Inside, the cabin was quaint but comfortable, with most amenities a person could want—three bedrooms, a large living room with a fireplace to help heat the place in the winter months, and a kitchen his grandparents had renovated when they'd decided to make the cabin their full-time home. By far the best feature of the whole place was the deck out back that went right up to the water line of Swinging Bridge Reservoir.

Not that he could enjoy the view of the lake like he had before the boating accident. Even after all this time, when he peered out over the water, he still felt sort of lost.

"Are you sure you're ready for this?" he asked, facing Olivia. She looked pretty in a modest V-neck shirt that brought out the gold flecks in her brown eyes, and jeans so skinny they could have been spandex. Not that he minded. He loved knee-high boots over jeans and she was definitely rocking that look.

She nodded and climbed out of the car. As she did, he noticed the lack of a panty line beneath her fitted jeans. *Another thong?*

Shaking his head to clear the vision of her naked flesh peeking out from under her pajama shirt the first night in his kitchen, he joined her on the front porch. Now was definitely not the time for thoughts like that, not when they had a Sunday family dinner to get through. Not when he had a room full of family to convince his relationship with Olivia was real. And definitely not when he was supposed to be thinking of her in a strictly business arrangement kind of way.

If only he could go back to that first night with her in his apartment and un-see her in that nightshirt, then things would be much easier. But, ever since he'd gotten a glimpse of her supple ivory skin, he hadn't been able to stop thinking about it, and somehow, those thoughts were starting to wander into dangerous territory—kissing, touching, longing.

So tempting. So forbidden. So off-limits.

"Is tonight going to be you and your cousin one upping each other to try to get the cabin? Should I say anything specific, or back you up in any particular way?" she asked, looking concerned.

"No. Once Gran and Gramps told us how they'd make their decision, there was no discussion. There's no point in trying to pitch our winning qualities to them. Our grandparents already know who we are and what we offer, and they'll make the decision they believe is right. The only thing you need to do is convince them that we're a couple, nothing more."

He slipped his hand around her waist, careful not to stray too low on her hip. She stiffened under his arm then peered up at him with nervousness in her eyes. He was taken aback by her closeness. If he bent down and she went up on her toes, their lips could meet somewhere in the middle for a kiss.

A kiss he couldn't allow to happen.

A kiss he didn't even want. Not really. No more than any man would want to kiss any beautiful woman. And she *was* beautiful.

She rubbed her shiny lips together as if checking to make sure they were still fully glossed. They were, in a warm color that made him think of cinnamon and sugar toast. Would she taste like cinnamon and sugar? Sweet and a little spicy?

She's Aidan's little sister.

He forced his thoughts back into safe territory. Obviously, this whole situation had thrown his hormones into overdrive. He'd never lived with a woman before. Even in this strictly platonic, business-arrangement-only way, having her in his space all the time was getting to him, especially when she paraded around half naked. That's all it was. A perfectly logical, guy's gut reaction to seeing a woman's bare ass in his kitchen. Nothing more.

Confident he'd unearthed the reason behind his sudden interest in Olivia, he put the whole thing out of his mind and hoped they looked like a couple in love and not like a couple of idiots trying to pull a fast one. Gran was tough and sharp, and she wouldn't be easily fooled. That was why they had to make this good. Believable.

They'd agreed earlier that touching was fine as long as it was kept to holding hands, arms around shoulders or waist, or hands on knees. Absolutely no kissing or neck nuzzling under any circumstances. They would convince his family they were a couple with their words and body language.

The door swung open and Gran yelled, "Sawyer's here!" She drew in a breath, a grin spreading across her face, making her eyes twinkle. "With a girl!"

"Gran…" His cheeks burned as he was pulled into the house, Olivia trailing after him. He didn't remember it being so hot inside, but today it felt as if it was the surface of the sun. He slipped his coat and hers from their shoulders and hung them in the front hall closet while Gran pulled Olivia into the living room.

She glanced back over her shoulder, mouthing the word, "Help."

He chuckled at her discomfort. At least he wasn't alone in the feeling.

Steeling his nerves for the onslaught of questions and teasing he knew was headed his way, he followed them into the living room. Olivia was already seated on the couch, iced tea in hand, sandwiched between Gran and his cousin's wife Sophia. The conversation was currently on Sophia's ever-expanding baby belly. She and Tyler were expecting their first in a few months and he wasn't sure who was more excited for the impending arrival—the soon-to-be parents, or Gran.

"Beer?" Gramps asked, handing him an unopened cold one.

"Absolutely. How are you feeling?" Sawyer asked before taking a drink.

Every time he looked at his grandfather, he couldn't shake the image of him lying in a hospital bed, sick with the flu and pneumonia that past winter. Thankfully, Gramps was strong, and with a dose of meds and a little rest, he'd kicked some serious illness ass. That didn't mean Sawyer could stop worrying that the outcome might be different next time.

"I'm doing well. I'd be even better if you'd stop treating me like I'm going to wither away and die every time I sneeze."

"Fair enough." He grinned.

"How're things with you?" Gramps asked, easing himself into the armchair in the corner.

"Good. Keeping busy." He took a swig of his beer, hoping it would help to take the edge off his nervousness.

"Too busy, I'm betting. Just like your father," his grandfather grumbled.

"You should talk," he quipped. Gramps had worked just as hard when he'd started the company. If Sawyer was anything like his father or Gramps, he could hold his head high and proud. A solid work ethic was not a fault.

"Found yourself a girl. Pretty one, too." Gramps tipped his beer toward Sawyer in a show of appreciation and took a deep chug.

"I did," Sawyer said. There was no point in denying her good looks, but that didn't mean he wanted to focus on them either. It was hard enough to ignore the stirrings she caused in his groin as it was.

"Didn't think I'd live to see the day you brought a girl home. She's the Morgans' girl, right?"

"Yep, Aidan's little sister." *Off-limits, remember?*

Aidan had gone so far as to call and lay down the rules concerning "fake dating" Olivia. Seemed he hadn't forgotten how Sawyer had hurt his ex-girlfriend Tammy by choosing work over her, and he heard Tammy still wasn't dating anyone because of the betrayal she felt. He wasn't about to see the same kind of hurt happen to Olivia. Therefore, there could be no line crossing, no gray area dating, no just-one-time flinging.

No groin stirrings allowed.

If he didn't follow the rules and ended up hurting Olivia, his friend had made it perfectly clear there'd be no friendship left. Aidan was more like a brother than a best friend, and there was no way Sawyer would risk losing another family member. He only had a few left.

"She went and grew up all of a sudden." Gramps clicked his tongue the way he always did when he saw something he liked, or hell, whenever Gran walked by. Old guy had the mind of a twenty-year-old.

"She certainly did," Sawyer said, eyeing Olivia. Rounded curves in all the right places, toned muscles, and a sexy spark of fire in her eyes—those things didn't even resemble the girl he used to know. Everything about her oozed savvy, street smarts, and sensibility. And sex. Every toss of her long hair felt like seduction, tempting him, teasing him.

Olivia still sat chatting happily with Gran, but Sophia was now puttering in the kitchen, putting the last few touches on dinner, no doubt. Gran and Gramp's house might be the central meeting place for dinner, but no one expected them to cook a feast. Instead, they took turns and this time it was his cousin's, which meant they were probably going to eat some kind of casserole and a salad. Sawyer didn't mind. As long as he didn't have to cook, everything tasted great. No one looked forward to his turn as chef.

"Dinner's ready," Sophia called from the dining area. It wasn't a typical formal dining room, but more of an extended eat-in kitchen.

As everyone headed toward the table, Sawyer made a beeline for Olivia, catching her hand, stopping her. She gazed up at him, her eyes giving away her surprise. He smiled lazily as if he were looking at a woman who'd offered to make pancakes at three in the morning instead of at the woman whose acting abilities held the future of his family's cabin.

"How are you holding up?" he asked, dropping his voice so only she could hear. He wrapped his hands around her waist, drawing her against him. If he wasn't mistaken, her eyelids fluttered for a moment before she responded.

"Great. Your family is wonderful." She pressed her hands to his chest. The heat from her palms penetrated his shirt in the most pleasant way. "I told them we reunited at dinner with Aidan after I got back into town and instantly hit it off. I think they bought it." She smiled sweetly up at him.

"Planning our story in advance was a good idea. You handled yourself really well, even with Gran's questions." Without thinking, he brushed his fingers along her cheek. Her skin was even softer than it looked. Her eyebrows rose with his intimate touch, but she didn't pull away. Instead he heard a tiny intake of breath as she licked her lips.

Damn those lips.

Every time he looked at them, he found them more and more intriguing. His thumb brushed against the corner of her mouth as her tongue swept past. A fraction of a second earlier and she would have licked his fingertip. A bolt of heat went through him at the idea of the other areas of his body where her tongue could explore. She wouldn't need a map; he'd inadvertently flagged the spot.

"Dinner's not getting any warmer, but if you two get any hotter we'll have to send you both straight to bed," Gran teased from the dining room doorway.

Sawyer took a step back and slipped his hand into Olivia's, laughing at his grandmother's terrible timing and dirty mind. "Gran, is that how you want to talk in front of Gramps?"

"Who do you think I learned it from? Your grandfather is no saint. In fact, he's a downright sinner in the bedroom and I love him for it." She laughed and wandered back into the dining room with a spritely spring in her step.

"My ears can't unhear that, Gran," Sawyer said with an amused chuckle.

"Think of how I felt," Tyler grumbled from the other side of the table. "I'm the one who had to fix their bedframe when a 'mysterious earthquake' rattled it too hard. I took half a day without pay to make sure they had somewhere to sleep that night."

Gran's cheeks pinked and Gramps' smile grew to a devious grin as they shared a knowing glance. "We don't know what you're talking about."

The comment from Tyler might have been funny to everyone else, but Sawyer couldn't ignore the undertone—it was Tyler who'd been there to help out Gran and Gramps when they needed it, not Sawyer.

Ever since Sawyer had taken over the business and moved into the city, it was his cousin who was nearby to lend a hand as needed, and he took every opportunity to mention how important he was to Gran and Gramps. But they were all Sawyer had left as "parents," and he wasn't about to let Tyler come between them, not now, not ever. He'd make sure to check and see if there was anything he could do before leaving tonight. After dinner, he'd ask Gran, privately.

Right now, he had to focus on convincing everyone he and Olivia were a real couple.

"Dinner will be interesting, won't it?" She whispered beside him. "Have we had sex yet?"

Sawyer stumbled and pulled her back against the wall outside the dining room. The mere mention of being with Olivia in that way sent his mind reeling. One palm pressed flat against the wall beside her head, blocking their faces from view, while his other cupped her jaw. His thumb stroked along the softness of her chin. His breath caught in his throat when he tried to speak quietly, his voice suddenly husky and filled with longing. "If we had, it'd be something you'd never forget."

Olivia had the nerve to roll her eyes at him. She was the one who'd brought up sex in the first place.

"I meant if they ask—which after Gran's comment seems likely—have we been intimate already? Is that something they would expect or frown upon?" She whispered into his ear, so close her warm breath simultaneously tickled and aroused him. "Have we banged or not?"

"Banged?" he asked, the corner of his lip curling. For

whatever reason, he'd expected her to be more innocent, a "we made sweet love" kind of girl. But perhaps she was more of a "quickie on the kitchen table" type.

He was totally okay with that. She kept getting more enticing.

"You know, slept together? Fooled around? Have we done it? I need to know how into you I'm supposed to be, since this is not a topic I expected Granny Sterling to bring up tonight." She sounded out of breath when she finally stopped talking. His gaze darted down to her chest as it rose and fell in quick succession. With every inhalation, her breasts strained against the fabric of her shirt and it took all of his willpower to pull his eyes away from those heaving mounds of temptation.

"If you're at dinner with my family, we've been there, done that. Multiple times. In one night." He grinned, letting himself indulge in the image of Olivia straddling his hips—naked, throwing her head back in pure ecstasy while she rode him, hard and uninhibited. "And in case you're wondering, it was fucking fantastic. The best you've ever had."

"Think pretty highly of yourself, don't you?" She tilted her head slightly, peering up at him. A twinkle of teasing flashed in her eyes.

"I've never had any complaints, sugar," he said, trying not to let her get under his skin.

"Too inexperienced to know the difference, were they?"

"Very funny."

She smirked. "I thought so, too."

He wanted to silence her smart-talking mouth with his, give her something to compliment instead of criticize. Sawyer brushed his thumb across her lower lip before trailing his hand down her neck. Stopping at her collarbone, he willed himself not to go any further. Not here. Not now.

No, not ever. Even if it had been on his mind since she walked into his apartment, and his life, almost a full week ago.

"I'm not going to tell you how to act, or force you to do anything you're not comfortable with." He fingered the pendant of her necklace where it dangled an inch above her cleavage. A little longer and the beautiful opal would be safely hidden between her luscious breasts, exactly where he'd like to find himself right now.

"But if anyone asks, I'm going to claim we've slept together already because if this was a normal situation and you were at Sunday dinner, we'd be one moment away from getting engaged."

For a second her demeanor changed from smiling, teasing, and flirting to sadness, pain, and longing. Before he could question her, she squared her shoulders, set her jaw, and the glimpse of raw emotion he'd seen a moment earlier disappeared entirely.

He took one last glance at the intriguing woman pressed between himself and the wall and wished she wasn't his best friend's little sister. All this discussion about having sex with her—even fictional, past tense sex—made his dick hot, heavy, and painfully confined.

With sudden clarity, he knew resisting her would be the hardest thing he'd ever done, but if he didn't, he put everything in jeopardy. He could unintentionally hurt Olivia, destroy his friendship with Aidan, and lose the only place he had to really call home. No woman was worth that much risk, not even temptingly sexy Olivia.

• • •

Olivia looked around the table, thoroughly enjoying the feeling of being part of a family again. She hadn't had a meal with both of her parents in the same room at the same time since their divorce. This feeling was welcome and what she wanted in her future—her own happy family.

She'd been silly to think for one second that Sawyer's family would grill them on the intimacy of their relationship. They were far too considerate to ask something so personal. They were mostly curious about her adventures around the world, and she'd spent more time talking than eating.

"So what will you be doing for work in the city?" Gran asked.

Olivia wiped her mouth with her napkin before answering. "Sawyer found me a job at Sterling Enterprises. It's not a permanent position, but it will give me plenty of time to figure out where I want to work and gain some experience for my resume."

"What kind of position is it? I thought Sterling was full," Tyler asked.

"It was until last week," Sawyer said. "Bethany had to take a sudden medical leave, which left us with an opening. Lucky for us, Olivia is more than qualified to do Bethany's job until she returns."

"Wonderful," Gran said. "And how nice that the two of you will get to work so closely together."

Would she have to work directly with Sawyer? Living in close proximity would be challenging enough, if every time he looked at her she got flustered. How would she manage working closely with him as well?

"It's not like her desk will be right in my office or any-thing," Sawyer said. "Not that it would really matter if it was. What's a little office space sharing, when we're already co-habitating, right?"

Sawyer placed his hand on her thigh for the fourth time since dinner started. Not that she was counting. She couldn't help noticing how quickly he'd forgotten their no touching above the knee rule.

She resisted the urge to squirm. The warmth of his touch sent another shot of liquid heat to the pressure building be-tween her legs, and it was everything she could do to ignore it. Regardless of how hard she tried, his touch, his smile—all of it—fanned a flame ignited deep inside.

When she'd agreed to this deal, she certainly hadn't tak-en time to think about all it would entail. Sure, saying they were dating was one thing, but acting like it was completely different. Acting like a fake couple shouldn't come with the very real feeling of his hand on her thigh, or the real reaction his touch caused.

"You're living together?" Gran asked, sounding surprised.

"Are you joking? The bachelor hooked up and shacked up?" Tyler probed.

"How unlike you," Sophia said.

"I…we shouldn't have… I'm sorry…" Seeing the ex-pressions on everyone's face made hers burn hot with em-barrassment. She'd assumed they'd be okay with their liv-ing arrangement, since it was Sawyer who'd suggested it. He could have warned her his family might take issue.

"You have nothing to be sorry for, sugar," Sawyer said. He took a sip of his beer as if this news was no big deal.

"Olivia moved in this week."

"Already?" Gran asked. "But you've only started dating. You're not even engaged yet. You barely know each other."

"That's my boy," Gramps cheered, tipping the neck of his beer bottle toward them like a salute.

Sawyer mimicked his grandfather's motion. "Thanks. Olivia may have only come back recently, but we have history together. It doesn't even matter that we haven't seen each other since…" He paused while taking an unsteady breath. "Since the accident. I feel like I've known her my whole life."

Olivia squeezed his hand. Hearing him mention the accident that had taken his parents' lives felt like a stab to her chest. From deep within the recesses of her mind, her parents' voices spoke, trying to comfort Sawyer shortly after it happened. She'd been listening from down the hall, sent to her room so they could have privacy, but she'd eavesdropped, and even though she hadn't seen his face, the torture in his voice had been vivid.

Sawyer squeezed her hand, too.

"You were probably sick of seeing me always tagging along with you and Aidan back then, huh?" she asked, trying to lighten the mood and ease the hard memories back into the past.

There was a smile on his lips, though she could see the pain still lingering in his eyes, still hear the twinge of sadness in his tone even as he tried to joke. "It's possible," he said with a chuckle. "But I was a kid and therefore can't be held responsible for my poor judgment."

Sawyer removed his hand from her thigh and slipped it around her shoulders instead. "We figured, why wait, you know? I've fallen hard for this one."

He pulled her close and she peered up at him with what she hoped was a convincing expression of adoration and love on her face. She was met by a smile that made her question if what he said was really an act.

That was a silly thought. Everything was an act. He had to make his family believe he'd found someone he could settle down with, or he'd never stand a chance to own the cabin. He was a good actor. She should take a lesson from him and stop feeling more than she was acting. Acting was safe. Feelings were trouble.

Gran's expression turned from surprise to happiness. "Why don't we have dessert and coffee in the living room?"

As they moved from the dining room, Olivia excused herself to use the bathroom. She didn't actually need to go. She simply wanted a few minutes alone.

Behind the safety of the bathroom door, Olivia closed her eyes and took a few deep breaths. Sawyer's hand on her body felt good, too good. She hadn't been prepared for how much touching would be involved in this scam. Tonight had been an eye-opening experience and, somehow, she would have to endure this kind of reaction to him every Sunday.

If his touch hadn't been enough, hearing him say he'd fallen for her had pushed her over the edge. She'd longed to hear a man say that. It was exactly what she'd hoped to find when she returned to the States. Of course, his words had only been pretend. Even though she knew that in her head, it didn't stop the rest of her body from responding to him as if it had been a truthful declaration.

"You need to get a grip on reality," she whispered to her reflection. Smoothing a few loose strands of hair behind her ear, she willed her nerves to steady and her hormones to chill. It was all an act, and she was not the one supposed to fall for it.

Olivia pulled open the bathroom door and stopped short of walking into Tyler. "Sorry, I'll get out of your way." She attempted to step around him but he moved, his broad shoulders and stocky build blocking her path. He was about the same height as her but twice the width, which made him come off as rather formidable.

"Actually, I had a question for you."

Something about his body language put her on the defensive.

"Ask me anything," she said, forcing a smile to her face. If she acted at ease, maybe she would feel at ease too.

"You and Sawyer, huh?"

Was that even a question, let alone one worth stopping her to ask?

"Yep," she replied simply.

"How'd that happen?"

"Oh, didn't you hear when I told your wife and Gran the story? I was staying with my brother Aidan when I first got back and he invited Sawyer and me out for dinner. I guess it was a love at first sight kind of thing." She shrugged. That sounded about the same as what she'd told the others. Sticking to the story would be hard if she had to keep repeating it.

Tyler narrowed his eyes, crossed his arms. "Funny how you could go from being such a free-spirited world traveler one minute to someone so domesticated the next."

"I guess that's how things—" She coughed, clearing her throat, which felt like it was closing. "I meant love. That's how love works."

"Sure it is. *Love* is a funny *thing*."

If no one else had given her a hard time, why the hell did he feel the need to cross-examine her? She held her gaze steady, not wanting to scan the room for Sawyer, as Tyler might read it as a sign of weakness.

"This wouldn't have anything to do with the deed, would it?"

"What deed?" she asked, playing dumb.

"Dating and living together and yet you don't know about the deed to the cabin? Interesting." His voice was thick with suspicion.

"The cabin? Of course I know about the deed to the cabin." She wouldn't let him leave thinking she and Sawyer weren't close enough for her to be involved in every detail of his life.

Before she could say anything else, Sawyer was at her side, his arm around her shoulders. The scent of sandalwood and something spicy surrounded her. Her body responded to his aroma, which made her head spin.

"I'd prefer you don't question my girlfriend for no good reason. If you're worried about the deed, that's your problem. Leave her out of it."

"I'm supposed to believe this is real? It's very convenient that your new relationship status happened to coincide with Gran and Gramps inferring they wanted to leave the cabin to someone who will have a family to share it with," Tyler said.

Sawyer tightened his arm around Olivia as if drawing strength from her. His smile was easy and casual and completely contradictory to how his body felt. "Fate works in mysterious ways, doesn't it, sugar?"

She smiled up at him lovingly. "It certainly does. I'm so glad fate brought us together when it did, because I can't imagine spending time with anyone but you."

Olivia rested her head on Sawyer's shoulder while her hand caressed his chest. She tried desperately to ignore the firm muscles beneath his shirt, but when her fingers accidently slipped between two buttons, a fine dusting of hair tickled her fingertips.

Tyler sighed in disgust. "Get a room. Isn't it enough Gran knows you're living together? You can't even manage to keep your hands off of each other here?"

As he walked away, Olivia felt Sawyer relax, and she turned to look up at him. She shifted back a step to give herself some much-needed distance from his tempting body and intoxicating aroma, but he held her close.

His hand traced a path up her spine to settle in her hair. His fingers grazed the nape of her neck and she tilted her chin up to him in an automatic response. He moved in, his lips drawing nearer.

When he glanced down at her, it was as if Tyler and the rest of the household had disappeared. Sawyer's gaze was intense. When he spoke again, she barely heard his words over her pulse as it drummed in her ears. "I think he bought it, but we can't be sure. Yet."

He pulled her tight against his body, her breasts pressing into his chest. She wrapped her arms around his waist and spread her hand flat on his lower back, grazing his belt. She fought the urge to dip her hands beneath the slick leather to explore what would no doubt be a perfectly sculpted rear.

Olivia opened her mouth to ask what else they could do to convince his family, but before she could whisper the words, his lips were on hers. She gasped, startled by his tongue as it slipped past her lips. All through dinner she'd fought the spark of arousal he'd caused with his touch, but his kiss set her insides on fire. Heat roared to life low in her belly, making her ache in a place that had been unattended for too long. When was the last time a man had merely kissed her and caused that kind of reaction? Never. Sawyer's kiss was unlike any other.

His tongue swirled around hers and she whimpered against him, almost pleading for him to stop and at the same time longing for him to continue. She should fight this intrusion and yet she encouraged him further by arching into him. Gripping the hem of his shirt, she tried to hold on to something tangible and real because this kiss was anything but that.

When he pulled back enough to nibble on her lower lip, her knees went weak and the only things she could focus on were the twinge of desire between her legs and the hard bulge in his pants pressing against her hip.

Finally, and all too soon, Sawyer pulled away from her, leaving her aching for more. Her eyes fluttered open and everything she felt inside herself was mirrored in his heated, half-lidded gaze.

How had this man, who was best friends with her brother—who was supposed to be her safety net from dating for the next few months—suddenly become the first guy to kiss her in a way that made her head swim and her body tremble? The relationship might be an act, but if that kiss was pretend, he deserved an Academy Award.

A throat cleared from somewhere in the room. Without leaving Sawyer's embrace, she turned to find eight stunned eyes watching them and four mouths gaping open like a school of guppies. Her cheeks burned with embarrassment when she realized Sawyer's family had witnessed their very public display of fake affection. She swallowed hard, unsure of what to say or do, but wanting nothing more than to magically disappear.

"Sugar, I think we've convinced them." His breath was warm on her earlobe and despite the fact that everyone was watching them, she couldn't stop from leaning into him, wanting more of his mouth on her body. He kissed her cheek then released her, his laugh breaking the silence in the room as if he wasn't as turned on by the intimacy as she was.

The erection nudging at her hip was proof he had been, but maybe that's all it was—a purely physical response to the stimulus of kissing her and not something deeper, more meaningful. His kiss could have been nothing more than part of the act and she'd let herself get carried away. Maybe the passion she thought she'd felt in his kiss was only in her head—her own wanting and wishing instead of actual fact and feeling.

She'd have to try harder not to let herself feel anything for Sawyer. Otherwise, if he planned on kissing her often, to convince his family their relationship was real, the next three months would be long and painful.

And sexually frustrating.

Chapter Four

That kiss…

Kissing Olivia had shaken him to the core.

It had been a necessity. Tyler had clearly been suspicious of them and it was the first thing Sawyer had thought of to convince his cousin. Never did he expect to be tricked by his own acting.

The kiss had been incredibly hot. He'd kissed a lot of women in his time, but none of them had made him feel the way she had. Where did he even start? It had been like eating filet mignon after mind-blowing sex, while drinking a twenty-five-year-old scotch. Her mouth had been inviting, encouraging, and sinfully captivating. If it hadn't been for someone in the room coughing, he could've kissed her all night.

The entire drive home, he'd done nothing but think of her. She'd been amazing at dinner. Charismatic, funny, sweet, engaging. She'd been everything he'd hoped and so much more, and since that spectacular kiss, she'd barely said two words to him.

It was time to break the silence. "Did you have fun tonight?"

"Yep," she answered quickly, still peering out the window.

Not the response he'd expected from the girl who chatted up his whole family for hours. "I think they really liked you. You seemed to fit in so easily. It's as if you're already a part of the family."

"Thanks." She smiled but it didn't reach her eyes. "They were wonderful. You're lucky to have such a great family."

He cringed at his own ignorance. Aidan hadn't kept it secret that his parents' divorce had turned messy and that family reunions were stressful. He hadn't even considered how she'd feel being in a family environment like Gran's house. "I guess I am. I never really thought of it that way since it's just my grandparents and cousins, not…parents or siblings."

"Parents are great, but not when they ship you back and forth every other holiday."

"So you must have loved your freedom while traveling. Going where you wanted, when you wanted."

"I did, for a while. The novelty wore off pretty quick, especially when I was around other families a lot. At this one village in Africa, I stayed with a nice family in their hut for a week. They fed and sheltered me and I helped out carrying water, scavenging for food, even assisting to build a hut for another family. That community had the fewest possessions I've ever seen, but they also had the most spirit. The day I left, the children gave me hugs, and I wanted so deeply to hug my own family, even if I had to go to multiple places to do so."

"It must have been an amazing experience. Life changing."

"It was. It made me appreciate everything I'd taken for granted before. I wish I could have dinner with my parents more often." Her voice was soft, almost sad.

"Me, too." What wouldn't he give for one dinner with his?

Finally, she turned to look at him as they pulled into a parking spot. Her brow was furrowed, her expression almost pained. Reaching out, she squeezed his hand where it rested on the gearshift between them. The warmth of her touch was nice, soothing, especially with the difficult reminder of his parents. "I'm sorry. I shouldn't complain about not seeing my parents when I can call them anytime I want."

"No need to apologize." He smiled, trying to make her feel better. "I get it. I'd want to spend time with my family if I could too, which is why I like Sunday dinners so much, despite the fact Tyler is always there."

"Every Sunday?"

"Twice a month usually." He shrugged. "But it's not exactly mandatory."

"Oh. Okay." She sighed.

It didn't sound okay. "Is there a reason you don't want to go?" He couldn't help feeling defensive. Like it or not, he needed this to work, and the Sunday dinners were the fastest way to convince his grandparents they were a legitimate couple. And his family was awesome, and had been nothing but wonderful to her. If she'd missed being a part of a family so much, why didn't she enjoy being a part of his?

She bit her lower lip, and memories of her mouth pressing against his flashed through his mind, banishing his annoyance. Her lips were naked now, free of the glossy color that had tinted their appearance and sweetened their flavor earlier. What would she taste like now?

Olivia put her hand up between them and he stopped his progression toward her. He hadn't even realized he'd been inching forward, but he had, pulled to her by some kind of invisible connection.

"This," Olivia said. "This is why I don't want to go."

"This what?" The fog filling his brain dissipated, replaced by irritation.

"Pretending to be your girlfriend is hard enough without all the extra kissing and touching and…" Her voice dropped off as she fled from the car toward the elevator.

Sawyer followed, trying to get his thoughts in order. She didn't like kissing him? But that kiss had been awesome.

He clenched his jaw to keep from speaking. Besides, what could he say? Apologize for kissing her after they'd talked about barely even touching in front of his family? Nope. He did what he had to do in the moment to convince Tyler, and he'd do it again in a heartbeat. Instinctively, his gaze went to her lips. The desire to kiss her—right here, right now—was almost overwhelming.

"We agreed to keep things as platonic as possible, but that kiss overstepped a few boundaries," she said.

"That kiss saved us from Tyler figuring out we're not for real." Sawyer moved across the tiny space of the elevator to hover in front of her. Besides, it wasn't like kissing her was torture—far from it. It had been nothing short of scorching hot. At least, that was how it had seemed to him.

"That kiss was unnecessary and it can't happen again." She raised her chin and met his gaze with ferocity. "We'll have to be more convincing in every other way, because I won't kiss you every time we have a family gathering."

Why wouldn't she kiss him? Was it because he was Aidan's best friend?

It didn't matter why. She was right. No more kissing allowed. She was Aidan's little sister and he wouldn't do anything to ruin his friendship. That kiss might have been fantastic, but it was also a huge mistake. Forcing himself away from temptation, he stepped back, putting space between them. She visibly relaxed, her shoulders slouching as she leaned her head back against the elevator wall.

How much clearer could her body language be?

She wasn't attracted to him, or as turned on by their kiss as he was. She'd played her part, nothing more, and even then she found it challenging. Isn't that what she'd said? Well, he wouldn't linger where he wasn't wanted.

He'd do whatever it took to make this work. The cabin was more important than hooking up with Olivia. He'd do what it took to keep things professional between them, starting now.

"I should be able to finalize everything at work tomorrow so you can start on Tuesday."

"Great," she said, sounding genuinely excited for exactly one second. "I guess I'll have to go shopping for work clothes. I hope my credit limit is high enough to buy a few outfits. I don't think you want me showing up in the denim cutoffs I wore to work at the pineapple plantation in Hawaii."

"Do you want an advance on your salary?" he asked, hating the thought that she was burdening herself to have something to wear to work.

She narrowed her eyes and pulled back her shoulders almost as if she were getting ready to duel. Had he offended her with the offer?

"I'll manage on my own," she said as they walked into the apartment.

"I don't doubt that you will." He hoped she heard the truth in his tone.

Olivia was stronger and more resourceful than any other woman he'd ever met. He had no doubt that if she set her mind to something, she would do whatever she had to until she achieved it.

He couldn't help but wonder if she put the same determination into her relationships. If the situation was different, and he made her want him, would she be as determined to succeed? Finding out was almost too tempting.

• • •

Olivia slapped her hand repeatedly against the black box making the offensive beeping sound. Enough. She got it. Time to get up.

After years of making her own schedule, falling back into the routine of a nine-to-five job was a huge adjustment, and one she wasn't necessarily ready for. She'd known the first week of her new job would be hard, but she felt as if she'd been woken from a coma. Every instinct she had whispered at her to roll over and go back to sleep.

She'd never been a morning person. Even back in her college days, she eventually got tired of showing up late and only scheduled afternoon classes. Getting to work everyday after lunch probably wouldn't go over well with Sawyer, even if they were living together—and fictitiously dating.

Throwing back the covers, she rolled to her feet then

staggered to the bathroom, rubbing her eyes. She paused in the doorway to stretch her arms above her head, twisting one way and then the other before pushing open the door, her eyes scrunched tightly closed against the blindingly bright vanity lights. Today was the first day of her new career, her new life. As she peeled her eyes open, gleaming white tiles and shiny counters assaulted her senses, but it was the object reflected in the mirror that really caught her attention.

Sawyer.

Naked.

Suddenly Olivia was very awake. Any trace of sleep-induced fogginess evaporated like steam from his hot shower.

His wet hair was spiked from a quick towel dry. A droplet of water ran down his bare chest, crested over the rolling hills of his pecs, skimmed the fine slopes of his six-pack abs like an Olympic mogul skier, then disappeared into a patch of dark hair below his belly button.

Nice.

The rest of him was covered by a towel, gripped in his hand, hanging in front of his groin like a big loincloth. A loincloth she'd love to see drop to the ground in a puddle around his feet.

Stop. It's Sawyer. Your boss.

Olivia had made the mistake of dating a boss in college, pre-asshole-Sam days, and it had ended about as well as a soap opera drama. Not only had she ruined her reputation, she'd lost a job she'd really needed. Playing the boss's girlfriend for a limited amount of time was one thing; becoming it in real life was completely another, and not something she'd ever risk again.

"Why didn't you lock the door?" she asked, forcing her

gaze to stay on his face.

"Why didn't you knock?"

"Because a closed door means nothing if it isn't locked. Haven't you ever had a roommate before?" She shook her head. "That's like Hostel Living 101."

"Sorry. I haven't had the opportunity to live the carefree hostel life. I've been busy running my business." There was no denying the edge in his voice. Nor could she ignore the sting of his words.

She'd worked while traveling, just a different kind of work. Apparently he didn't get that, like the rest of the businesses in this city that wouldn't hire her. Why had he even bothered offering her a job if he felt her work ethic wasn't worthy of the position? Oh right, because of the cabin. His needs were met; hers were a bargaining chip. It wasn't as if she'd earned the job by being the best applicant.

The edge of his towel swayed as he rotated it to wrap the material around his waist. He ran his hands through his hair, looking frustrated, before shrugging. "I'm decent now, and we're running late, so you better get moving."

Even Olivia's irritation and tiredness couldn't stop her from noticing that Sawyer was far more than decent. His lower half might be hidden from view, but the upper gave her an eyeful. Calling his chest merely decent should be illegal. The term was an injustice to the sculpted muscles and fine dusting of hair. The bathroom tiles were decent. Sawyer, on the other hand, was fantastic. And he was smirking at her.

"What?" she asked, suddenly feeling like she'd been caught peeking at Christmas presents, but she resisted the urge to shrink back into her room. Instead she stood her ground confidently.

"Nothing." He grinned.

"If it's nothing, then why are you looking at me that way?" she asked, hands on her hips.

"I'm the one who should be asking that question, don't you think? I was minding my own business, taking a shower, when you barged in. And had a pretty good look around while you were at it."

"I…" What could she say? That she hadn't seen anything? She had. *A really good something.* "I'm sorry I walked in without knocking. I saw nothing… Well, not nothing, exactly. I mean I saw all that." She motioned to his chest then dropped her gaze to his towel again. "But nothing important like *that*."

Shut up!

"Sorry, I'm kind of out of it today."

"Didn't you sleep well?" Concern wrinkled his brow.

The notion he'd be concerned about her comfort level made her insides soften. How long had it been since anyone—especially a guy—cared about her daily well-being? Not since she'd left home for college. She'd been on her own a long time. "I slept fine. I'm not used to getting up early." The look on his face said he wanted to roll his eyes.

"Well, get used to it because the office opens at nine every morning, no exceptions."

She couldn't tell by his tone if he was really warning her like a boss or if he was simply teasing her like a boyfriend. But then, he wasn't a boyfriend, only a pretend boyfriend, when they were in public. And they most certainly weren't in public right now. Nope. Just a private bathroom with a guy who was still very naked under his towel.

"I promise I'll get it together and I'll be up and at work

on time every morning." He'd given her a job when no one else would, and she wasn't about to screw up the opportunity to have Sterling Enterprises on her resume, just because she liked to sleep in.

Sawyer said some words that sounded like he'd muttered them underwater, then crossed his arms in front of his chest. His biceps swelled. "Won't you?"

What was that now?

"Yes?" she replied, confused but not wanting to admit it. All she could focus on were the flexed biceps teasing her from across the room, taunting her to touch them, climb them, wrap herself in them.

No, no, no, no, no. No. I mean it. No.

She shouldn't be attracted to him. One, he'd just been a jerk, accused her of barging into the bathroom—which she sort of had, but whatever—and hurt her feelings about her work ethic for the last five years. Two, he was her new boss, and she wasn't going down that road again. Three, he was her brother's friend, which would mean bad news for them. And four, she was off the market for the next three months, at least, to everyone, including—and especially—Sawyer.

If only he'd go put some damn clothes on, maybe she'd even be able to remember all those reasons for longer than a nanosecond.

"Great. I think that would be best since I need to show you around the office. Well, and because it won't be a secret we're dating."

Could he bench-press me? They do that sometimes in movies. Always looked silly, but now… Maybe.

She couldn't believe only two short days ago those strong arms had been wrapped around her while he'd kissed her in front of his family. She hadn't appreciated them nearly enough. She'd known, in the moment, that he was muscular, but seeing him up close and personal, and in the flesh, left no doubt about how built he was. He could probably do a hundred pushups without breaking a sweat. That kind of arm strength could come in real handy if he were hovering over her...in bed...while inching into her.

"Olivia." Sawyer's voice was strong and commanding.

She could think of a few commands she'd like to hear in that voice. *Lay back. Kiss me.* The thought of Sawyer dominating her in the bedroom was enough to make her knees weak. She gripped the side of the doorframe to steady herself.

"Are you okay?" he asked, reaching for her. As he stepped forward, his hips strained against the towel tied at his waist. *Please fall.*

She held out her hand to stop him. "I'm fine. Just having trouble waking up." *And having trouble ignoring the naked hunk in front of me.* The one who she wasn't supposed to develop any kind of real feelings for, but who was making it hard when he was so damn sexy all the time.

"Maybe you should get in the shower." He stopped at the door to his room. "Will you be ready to leave in a half hour? So we can drive together, like I asked."

Drive together! She nodded. That's what he'd been saying. Sure. Fine. Good.

He disappeared into his room and she locked the door behind him. It was one thing to see him half naked, but she wasn't ready to return the favor yet.

Not if she wanted to stay true to their plan.

Chapter Five

"I guess you didn't have any trouble finding work attire," Sawyer said, hitting the appropriate button. She didn't miss his sideways glance raking up her body from the toe of her new knee-high boots to the top of her cowl-neck blouse.

Her shoulders relaxed. Good. She'd been worried that the pinstriped pencil skirt with the slit up the side would be too risqué for Sterling Enterprises.

"Candace," he said to the receptionist at the front counter. "This is Olivia. She's filling in for Bethany."

"Is this your…" Candace's voice trailed off.

He put his arm around Olivia's shoulders in a way that felt both loving and professional. "Yes, she's my girlfriend."

Candace beamed. "I didn't actually think you existed. But here you are!"

"You thought I made up a girlfriend?" he asked, showing surprise with a hint of annoyance.

"I want to hear all about your travels around the world."

Candace practically wiggled in her seat.

"It's nice to meet you," Olivia said, genuinely happy. Having someone to take coffee breaks with would make settling in so much easier. "I guess Sawyer mentioned what I've been up to for the last few years."

"He did. I can't wait to pick your brain about the places you've been. Coffee later?" she asked.

"Let's get Olivia settled before you start drilling her with questions." Sawyer walked off, but hadn't even made it a few steps before Candace spoke again.

"If you're going to her desk, you're headed in the wrong direction. Yesterday, Matt and Susan decided she should be close by to help you with the Marcus project."

Why couldn't she be on opposite side of the office and still work on the project?

Sawyer smiled, but it looked half-hearted. Maybe he wasn't thrilled about working so closely with her either. "Great," he said with a half smile. "Let's go see where you'll be sitting."

Sawyer introduced her to the team as they walked past their offices. Everyone seemed very welcoming and warm. She'd never worked in an office like this, but the response felt above and beyond the norm.

More than once, she'd seen the look of surprise when Sawyer introduced her as his girlfriend. Either Sawyer had never dated anyone at work before, which was probably a good thing since he was the boss, or he had simply never had an actual girlfriend. She speculated that both instances were true.

When they'd finally made it to his corner office—with a view of the park—they'd also inadvertently found her desk—right outside his door.

Thanks to her degree in business and minor in communication, Matt and Susan had apparently deemed her too important to be far away. Not only would she be overseeing light administrative tasks as needed, but she'd be helping Sawyer to come up with marketing strategies for the new vitamin-enriched products Todd Marcus wanted to introduce to the world.

From her chair, Sawyer was in plain view. For the hundredth time that day already, she peeked up through her lashes to where he sat at his desk, looking incredibly tempting and forbidden. She couldn't help it. The man looked damn good in a suit. But he was off-limits, and for so many good reasons. He was Aidan's friend. He was a player, not a settling down kind of guy. He was the kind of guy who would never change—just like Sam, ex-fiancé extraordinaire—the kind of guy who was the exact opposite of what she wanted in her future. And the attraction that had been sparking between them was spurred by their required acting skills. Nothing more.

That didn't seem to deter her from eyeing him as if he alone was the answer to the ache throbbing low in her belly. She tried to stop herself, to focus on her tasks, to learn her new position, but it was challenging. Knowing Sawyer wasn't a viable option in her life was one thing, but telling her body to shut up and listen to reason was another thing completely. Not to mention, he didn't seem the least bit bothered by having her nearby. He'd been clicking away on his computer all morning, rarely glancing up or moving. The man was a machine. She was curious to see if he'd even take a lunch break.

"Olivia," Sawyer called, glancing up to find her staring at him.

She startled, almost spilling her coffee. "Yes?"

"I'm printing off a few things. Would you mind getting them?"

"Not at all." While she waited for the documents to finish printing, she cursed herself for having been caught staring at him. She'd have to get her act together if she wanted to do her job properly, and if she wanted to maintain their strictly *business* arrangement.

It hadn't been that long since she'd been intimate with someone, had it? *Paris,* she thought, recalling her last encounter. The city of love. And quickies. She'd met someone at the Louvre, then had a coffee and a quick romp back at his place. It had been intense, spontaneous, and totally stupid. It had also been almost a year ago.

A year? That explained a lot.

When the machine finally fell silent, she grabbed the printouts and headed back to Sawyer's office. He motioned to the chairs in front of his desk. "Have a seat."

They lived together and were supposed to be dating, yet when she sat there with him, her pulse raced. He might only be her fake boyfriend, but he was her very real boss, and she needed to make a good impression if she was going to earn a reference.

Sawyer shuffled through the pages then handed her a few. "This is some basic research for the Marcus project. It's my top priority. Between your degree and your world travel, Matt and Susan believe you can offer a fresh perspective on this client and his needs. After reviewing everything we have so far, I'm inclined to agree with them."

"I'm happy to help in any way I can."

Sawyer's desire and drive to make his company success-ful was obvious, and working with a man who was passion-ate about his business was really exciting…and sexy too.

"I'm glad to hear that. I think the best place to start is to familiarize yourself with the company, their history, their product, and their goals."

"I can do that," she said.

"Keep in mind we're creating an international marketing strategy, since this is a global product launch."

She nodded. *Sure, global. I took a class for that in school. I must remember something from it.* "Absolutely. No prob-lem." She wasn't entirely confident, but how hard could it be?

"What we're really hoping for is any insight you can pro-vide about the different cultures you experienced. Like the story you told me about that village in Africa. Make notes of how other cultures could incorporate the products into their daily lives. Okay?"

Wow. Nothing like being asked to perform on command.

"Sure." Olivia twisted her hands together in her lap, be-low the level of the desk, where he couldn't see. Maybe this job was a tiny bit over her head. But sink or swim, right? She couldn't afford to sink, so she'd have to brush up on her global marketing skills and figure it out. She must've expe-rienced *something* while traveling that would be applicable.

She glanced up to find Sawyer watching her, eagerness, excitement, and drive vibrating through every inch of his body. He'd given her an opportunity and she wouldn't waste it with self-doubt. She'd promised herself she'd do whatever it took to get her future on the right path. Now was the time to pull her shit together, take each task in turn, and make this job a success.

"I'll get started on this right after lunch," she said, shuffling the papers around while trying not to worry.

"Is it lunchtime already?" he asked, glancing at his watch.

"Want to grab a quick bite with me? I'm not sure what's close by."

"Can't. Too much to do."

"Where's your favorite place?"

He chewed the end of a pen for a moment before answering. "You know, I can't remember the last place I had lunch where I wasn't at a business meeting uptown. Candace is really your best bet for insider information on places to eat."

"You should take a break. It's not good for your body to sit and chug coffee all day." Seriously, did he leave his desk for more than bathroom breaks and coffee refills?

"I don't chug my coffee. And I get all the exercise I need playing soccer in the evenings. *After* work."

She narrowed her eyes at his stubbornness. Maybe he was more like his father than she realized—workaholic to the extreme. "I'm merely suggesting that you take care of yourself as well as you take care of your clients. I thought with your family history, you'd realize how important it is."

"My family history is not your concern. Besides, you can't fight your fate. Genes are genes." His tone was stiff and his comment seemed stilted. Then, in the next instant, his entire demeanor changed, relaxed. "But if you're insisting, I'd love it if you'd bring me back a bite to eat. Thanks so much for taking care of me, sugar."

Sugar? He hadn't called her that since their family dinner. Apparently the pet name would be making appearance at work, too.

"Matt," Sawyer said, his voice filled with confident professionalism again. "What can I do for you?"

Matt strode through the doorway and sat in the chair next to hers. So the "sugar" comment was part of the act.

"I need to run through some numbers with you."

"Sure, no problem. Olivia was just running out to lunch. Have you two met yet?"

"We have," Olivia said. "We met in the break room earlier, when Candace showed me how to work the coffee machine."

"Never used one before?" The comment felt like a dig to her inadequacies in the workplace. Or maybe she was overly sensitive.

"No. Unfortunately, I had to grab whatever I could find, wherever I was. I have to say, I much prefer this method of getting my caffeine fix."

"I'm sure you had all kinds of amazing local delicacies. I can't wait to hear about them sometime." Matt flipped open the file folder in his lap.

"Why don't I leave you to it?" Olivia was at the door when Sawyer spoke again.

"Aidan texted me earlier. He wants us to join him for dinner. We don't have anything planned, do we, sugar?"

There it was again. The first time he'd "sugared" her, she'd been too surprised to soak it in. But this time the endearment settled over her like a warm blanket on a cold night. It heated her skin, making her feel lightheaded. Not the response she was supposed to feel for Sawyer, at the office or anywhere else.

"Dinner sounds great." She hoped it came off as natural because it certainly didn't feel that way.

She dropped off the papers at her desk and grabbed her handbag. Sawyer might put work before everything else, but if she was in charge of his lunch, then damn it, he would be eating something healthy. Maybe next time he'd take a short break to join her. This time, though, a quiet lunch alone would help her think of some ideas for the Marcus project.

Chapter Six

Sawyer ordered a pint of the beer on tap and closed his menu. Tonight was definitely a steak kind of night. He needed the spike of energy the red meat would give him after the long day at work.

"I wonder where Aidan is," Olivia said setting her menu on top of his.

"It's not like him to be late. Maybe he got held up at work."

"Or maybe he's ditched us for better company." Olivia's smile told him she was joking.

He liked hanging out with someone who wasn't serious all the time. So many of the girls he'd been with in the past were pretty lackluster once the alcohol stopped flowing. Olivia was one of the few who could hold up her end of the conversation and do it with style, smarts, and sarcasm. The combo was a definite turn-on.

"Better company than his best friend and his adoring

little sister? Never." Little sister hung in the air between them. No matter how much he enjoyed her company, or how attracted he was to her, she was still a fake date.

No real relationship. No real ties. No real feelings.

If only it wasn't so exhausting trying to remember that all the time. He shifted in the booth. His whole body ached from tension, as if he'd run a marathon instead of having an average day at work. But maybe that's because it wasn't exactly average.

Not with Olivia around.

He'd expended more energy trying not to watch her all day than he had on actually accomplishing work. It had been exhausting, staring at a computer screen but not seeing a single idea through to fruition. Olivia in work clothes could definitely be considered a distraction. There was something so sexy about her business attire. The whole boss/secretary fantasy flitted through his mind—her lying across his desk, skirt pushed up her thighs, blouse open, and breasts exposed.

He stifled a groan. Tomorrow, he'd get back into his normal work groove. Now was not the time to let his work slide, or his entire company would suffer. He wanted nothing more than to leave work at work, but he couldn't. "Listen, about what happened in my office today—"

"I never should have bothered you about not eating or about working too much. How you spend your day is your business, not mine."

"If you'd let me finish, I was going to say thank you for playing along and fetching me lunch. I would never normally ask you to, but when I saw Matt walk up, it was the first thing I thought of that sounded sort of boyfriend-y."

"I didn't mind. I was just happy to know you got

something to eat and had more than just coffee to drink."
She bit her lower lip, looking guilty. And sexy. "Did you enjoy your spinach salad and kale chips?"

"They were awful and not nearly coffee-flavored enough."
Seriously, kale and chips should never be combined in any
form.

"You're welcome." She laughed and her energy lit up
her eyes, making them sparkle.

Leaning across the corner of the table, he slipped his
hand around the nape of her neck and peered into her eyes.
This time, her concern didn't aggravate him. It was kind of
sweet, endearing—it triggered something unfamiliar inside
him.

He'd let his stubbornness take the front seat, and as a re-
sult, Olivia had left his office feeling chastised for wanting to
do something good for him. Had he ever done that to other
employees without knowing it? Maybe his business was failing because he was a shitty boss.

If he'd done this to anyone else at work, made anyone
else feel this way, he would be annoyed at himself. But the
fact that it was Olivia ate at his insides. Maybe it was because she was his friend's little sister and he felt the need to
protect her.

He feared it was something more.

Kissing her had sparked something deep in his soul and
he hadn't felt right since. And the way she'd looked at him
afterward had spoiled him for any other expression. He'd
seen happiness and desire in her eyes, and now seeing anything else was a sword to his chest.

"I'm sorry I overreacted at work. I've been stressed. The
truth is, if this Marcus project doesn't come through, I might

have to shut the doors to Sterling Enterprises."

"Tell me how I can help, and I'll try my best."

He knew she would. No one could travel and work with only a backpack for five years without setting a goal and making it happen. "I'm hoping you can share some of your traveling experiences so we get a glimpse into what life is like for the people we'll be marketing to in other countries."

She put her hand on his knee and gently squeezed it, as if to comfort him.

She did. More than she probably realized. More than he expected.

She smiled and it was the best thing he'd seen all evening. "That I can do." Her tongue darted out to give her lips a quick lick and he was overcome with the desire to kiss her, right there, right then. Not because someone was watching and they were performing, but because he wanted to.

"I hope you're not acting like that on my account." Aidan took his seat across the table. "Actually, I hope you are acting because if this is a real moment I'm witnessing, then you leave me no choice but to take you outside to kick your ass."

Her gaze flickered down to his lips. Sawyer sank into his chair, leaving his hand on the back of her neck for another moment, not wanting to stop touching her.

"Relax. We're chatting about work." Sawyer sighed and gripped his cold glass instead of Olivia, already missing the feel of her warm, soft skin under his fingertips.

"I don't know, from my angle it looked like you two were getting awfully cozy. Don't tell me I've made a huge mistake letting this arrangement happen."

"Last time I checked, you weren't involved in the

arrangement between us." She raised her chin.

"Is that right?"

"The lady has spoken." Sawyer smirked. He liked having her on his side. Not that he was against Aidan in any way, but having her defend their agreement felt surprisingly good. For once, he wasn't alone in trying to reach his goals.

Olivia covered her mouth as she yawned. "I know you guys are used to working but I'm not and my first day was exhausting. I don't want to argue. I want to sit here, have a drink and a bite to eat, possibly some good conversation—although with you two, you'll probably have me bored to tears—and then you're taking me home to bed."

The beer hit the back of Sawyer's throat when he inhaled quickly at her unexpected words. He coughed and covered his mouth with his napkin. Her cheeks turned bright red.

"That's not what I meant," she said. "I meant he drove us here so after dinner, technically, he'd be the one taking me home. And then I intend to go straight between the sheets."

Sawyer arched an eyebrow and couldn't hold back a smirk.

"Really?" Aidan asked, chuckling.

"Alone. I'm going to bed *alone*. So I'm not tired for work tomorrow." She scoffed at both of them in turn. "You two have your minds in the gutter. And gross. You're my brother, he's your best friend. You should kick his ass right now for being a part of this conversation."

They laughed while she rolled her eyes.

They dug into their meals, eating in silence for a few minutes. Sawyer's steak was tender and juicy and exactly the taste he'd been looking for, but he had to admit, Olivia's pasta looked delicious. Or maybe it was the way she licked her plump, pink lips after every bite.

"I know you haven't been on a regular schedule in a while, but getting up today couldn't have been that hard," Aidan said.

"I'll get used to it. After this morning's incident, I'm not about to risk being overtired again. Tonight I'm going to bed at a decent hour and tomorrow my alarm will be set for fifteen minutes earlier so I can sufficiently wake up before it's my turn to in the bathroom." Olivia glanced around the room before continuing. "Speaking of the bathroom, I'm going to find the Ladies."

Remembering the incident made him wish the tables had been turned that morning. He'd love to walk in on her getting out of the shower, her body slick with water, her hair messy and hanging free over her naked shoulders.

"What happened this morning?" Aidan asked, grinning like he was about to hear a juicy story. Sawyer was pretty sure he'd feel differently in about thirty seconds.

"Your sister may have walked in on me getting out of the shower, but I was covered by a towel. Mostly." He laughed as Aidan's grin slid into a sneer. "Don't worry. Her virtue is still intact. Or if it isn't, it wasn't my fault."

"Let's leave my virtue, or lack thereof, out of conversations with my brother." Her hips swayed tantalizingly as she walked away. The curve of her muscular calves drew his attention to her legs—all the way up to where they disappeared beneath her skirt.

"Done ogling my sister yet, douche?" Aidan's fist connected with Sawyer's shoulder in a way that went beyond playful. "Eyes forward."

"I can't help it if she has a great body. I'm like a

connoisseur of art, I might admire the masterpieces, but that doesn't mean I'm going to buy one and take it home."

"Don't let me stop you from admiring whatever art you enjoy, but when it's attached to my sister, hands off. That Sam kid really hurt her when he dumped her—practically at the altar—back in college, and I'm not about to let you come anywhere near hurting her too. I lost her for five years while she sorted out her issues and now that she's back, I'm not going to let you send her running away again. Got it?"

"Shit. I forgot about that." He paused, considering Aidan's information. "Don't worry. I have no plans for putting my hands on your sister unless it's absolutely necessary to get the cabin. Otherwise, it's strictly business."

Why did he feel as if he'd lied under oath?

"It better be." Aidan relaxed into his chair, the tension clearly leaving. "How's the cabin project coming along?"

"Not as well as I'd hoped. When we were there this weekend Tyler mentioned all the work he's done around there to help them out. Of course he wouldn't miss an opportunity to point out his dedication to the cabin, and my lack of it, while rubbing his relationship with Gran and Gramps in my face." Sawyer sighed. "I have to figure out a way to do the same."

"To stoop to his level?"

"If it gets me the cabin, it'll be worth it in the end."

"So go out there and fix something."

"There's nothing that needs fixing until we do the usual seasonal stuff. Maybe I can order new window screens or something. We've been patching the current ones for years."

"That could work. Possibly expensive, but makes a statement. Although, it's an expense your arch nemesis might be the one to benefit from in the end."

Before he could say more, Olivia came back to the table.

"What did I miss? You two look very serious all of a sudden."

"Nothing." They both spoke at the same time.

"Talking about ordering new window screens for the cabin," Sawyer added.

"Fun." Her voice was thick with sarcasm. "Nothing like throwing a little money around to show someone you care."

Her complete and utter flippancy about the whole subject irked him. How was it she could get under his skin one minute then be awesome the next? Was she like this when they were younger, too, and he'd forgotten that part of her personality?

"Well, I have to do something to counteract Tyler's handyman status around my grandparents. Got a better idea?"

She shrugged. "Call me crazy, but you could tell them how much the cabin means to you. Surely they'd give you some extra consideration because you practically grew up within those walls."

"You think I want their pity vote?" Now he'd gone from irked to irate.

She put her hand on his and squeezed it. "I only meant that maybe you don't need to worry so much or try so hard because you already have more attachment and right to the cabin than Tyler."

"Tell that to the guy who's been working on the cabin damn near every month since I moved out a couple of years ago." He rolled his hand under hers so their palms pressed together. The sensation of her touch sent warmth blooming in his chest, melting away his irritation.

Aidan reached across the table and put his hand on top of theirs. "This is nice. We should all hold hands as *friends* more often."

Sawyer sat back and folded his arms across his chest, refusing to meet his friend's gaze. He cleared his throat before continuing. "It's not that I don't want to be the one to do the work, but it's too hard to make it out to the Catskills every weekend, which is why we only have Sunday dinners once or twice a month."

"So order the screens then. They do need them and I'm sure they'll appreciate the gesture."

"We should do something to celebrate your first day at work." Aidan smiled in what Sawyer recognized as his friend's getting-out-of-trouble face, which he used every time a conversation needed a quick change of topic.

"Dessert?" she asked.

"Perfect." Sawyer nodded, then waved over the server and requested to see the dessert tray. After perusing their options, they made their selections. "Do you have any specialty coffees?"

"We do offer a variety of coffees with liquors in them that pair well with the desserts. I would suggest either the Irish kiss if you like it hot or the chocolate orgasm if you'd prefer a cold drink."

"What do you think? Kiss or orgasm?" Sawyer asked, trying not to laugh. He'd just been told to watch it around Olivia and now here he was, offering her two deliciously inappropriate treats.

"I'll have an Irish kiss. I like my coffee hot."

Sawyer liked things hot, too. "I'll have that as well. Aidan?"

"Just a regular coffee for me. I've got work to finish at home."

"And one little drink is going to change that? We've only missed one weekend at the bar. Surely you can't be a lightweight already."

"No worries. I could still drink you under the table. But tonight I'm running numbers and that pesky decimal point tends to jump around if I have too many."

Their coffees arrived, along with dessert, and Olivia was the first to try her Irish kiss. When she emerged from behind the large mug, her top lip was coated in a layer of whipped cream. Sawyer reached out to wipe it away with his thumb but before he could, her tongue did the job for him.

The ache in his groin intensified. He stifled a groan, knowing there would be no relief for his growing needs tonight, or any other night in the near future...not unless he took care of business solo-style. After witnessing Olivia's tongue licking her lips clean, he knew his hand would never compare.

Note to self: ordering drinks topped with whipped cream is bad for my balls.

Chapter Seven

Olivia tried to read the numbers on the elevator control panel as they glowed, but each digit seemed to dance before her eyes. Speaking of dancing, the normally stationary walls seemed to be sashaying to music she couldn't hear.

"You doing okay?" Sawyer asked. His strong, steady grip on her arm hadn't faltered since they'd left the restaurant.

"Fine," she said, trying to sound convincing.

When did I become such a lightweight?

She hadn't had that much to drink. Two little glasses of wine with dinner and then the Irish kiss with dessert.

Irish kiss… Is Sawyer Irish?

Her gaze dropped to his lips…lips practically begging her to kiss them.

There was that grin again.

If she could get to her room and into bed, tonight would be over. The problem was, she needed Sawyer to help her get there, and every second his hand lingered on her arm, she imagined it lingering somewhere else on her body, somewhere she shouldn't be thinking about.

"I can handle my liquor, you know."

"You can, huh?" Sawyer let go of her arm and she breathed a sigh of relief. Now if he would also take a step back. His proximity made it harder to think clearly.

"What would your boss say if he knew you were getting drunk on a work night?" he asked.

"Probably nothing, since it's hard to discipline an employee when you're guilty of the same offense, don't you think?"

"You might be right." Sawyer finally took a small step back, giving her room to breathe without the intoxicating scent of his cologne. "What if the boss is fine in the morning but the employee is hung over?"

"If the boss was a nice employer, he'd fix the employee a cup of coffee and turn the other cheek, cutting said employee a little slack for celebrating her first day of work. At his recommendation, I would add."

"Good thing your boss is a very nice and understanding man."

The elevator chimed and jolted to a stop. Olivia's knees buckled and she reached out to brace herself. His arm slipped around her waist, holding her steady.

"I've got you," he said, guiding her down the hall to their apartment.

"I said I was fine."

"Yes, you did, and the evidence clearly shows that as well, doesn't it?" He glanced down at her while unlocking the door.

She narrowed her eyes. "You're more of a smart ass than

I remember."

"I'm surprised you remember my ass."

"We were kids, and that wasn't what I meant."

"No?" he asked, his voice rising as if he were teasing.

"I meant you're mouthier than I remember." First she'd mentioned his ass, now his mouth. She needed to stop speaking before she brought up any other body parts. All of them were on her mind.

Sawyer stopped outside her bedroom door, his hands lingering on her hips as she turned her back to the wall, leaning on it for support.

His mouth turned up at the corner. "I can be very mouthy, when asked nicely." His eyes held a devious glint that matched his suddenly husky tone. Maybe she wanted to follow his train of thought for a while, see where it led.

She could definitely get onboard with his mouth leading to hers right about then. The first time they'd kissed, something inside of her had threatened to explode, and that was with an audience watching. What would it be like if he kissed her, there, in the privacy of their home?

"Oh?"

He mumbled an unintelligible response as he shifted against her, pressing her back to the wall. She squirmed against the pressure building in the junction of her thighs and the growing evidence of his erection nudging her belly.

She parted her lips in silent invitation, even as her brain yelled for her to stop, begging her to listen to reason. Reason was a negative bitch, whereas spontaneity was a hungry vixen ready to get her fix.

Sawyer was gorgeous from a distance, but up close and personal, he was unbelievably sexy. Every inch of him was a temptation to her senses, and she wanted nothing more than to touch him, taste him, feel his tongue explore her mouth and body.

Aidan's annoying threats arose from somewhere inside her mind, warning her to stay away from Sawyer, the player, a guy who was just like Sam. A guy who wanted no future like the one she saw for herself. She shoved Aidan's voice into the darkest regions of her consciousness.

Screw her brother. If he got mad at her because she kissed a guy, he would get over it. She was a grown woman and she could kiss whomever she wanted, even if that someone was a playboy like Sawyer. Especially if it was Sawyer.

Sawyer didn't have to be a forever kind of guy. They were playing the role of a couple for everyone else. Maybe they could call another kiss practice. She'd like to practice.

Slipping her hands around his waist, she pulled him tight to her body and peered up at him. In an instant, his thumb was stroking her lips. She gasped at the contact, arching into him, letting her eyelids flutter closed so she could focus on his touch.

"Oh God, Olivia. I want…" His voice trailed off when she flicked her tongue against the tip of his thumb, urging him to taste her.

"You want what?" she asked, whispering.

"I want…you," he whispered back. His forehead rested on hers and his hand dropped to her shoulder, squeezing it as if he might draw strength from her.

She tilted her head slightly, offering herself.

"But I can't." A moment later, he closed his bedroom door, leaving her alone in the hall, trembling with need.

She changed into her pajamas while trying not to fall

over, then climbed into bed and pulled the blankets around her, desperately hoping to block out the rest of the world. He acted like he was as into the almost-kiss as she was, but when it came right down to it, he'd walked away.

What kind of playboy walked away from a woman offering herself to him? What kind of self-respecting, independent woman offers herself to a man who she knows is nothing but trouble? Hadn't she learned her lesson in college?

She groaned and rolled onto her side, cuddling her covers in her arms. Tears of embarrassment and rejection, past and present, stung her eyes.

They had an agreement, an arrangement to keep things above board and platonic—friends-only zone. Then she'd gotten drunk and crossed the line. She'd thought he'd looked at her with desire in his eyes.

She wouldn't be stupid enough to make that mistake again.

• • •

"Wake up. It's your turn in the shower," Sawyer said, brushing her hair away from her eyes. "If you don't get up now, we'll be late."

He knelt at the side of her bed, debating. A part of him—the part that saw how intoxicated she was last night, the part also feeling partially responsible for her current state—wanted to leave her in bed to sleep it off. But the other part of him, the boss part, knew missing her second day of work without a good excuse would only make her look irresponsible.

He shook her shoulder gently.

She stirred and rolled over onto her back, her blankets slipping down to her abdomen. Raising her arms above her head, she stretched, long and liquid like a cat waking from an afternoon nap in a sunbeam. As she did, her breasts strained against the thin material of her tank top pajamas.

The two luscious mounds looked like the perfect handful. Usually his philosophy was the bigger the boobs the better, but hers were perfect. Any bigger and they would have looked unnatural. The ribbed material of her tank must have rubbed against her nipples since they were beading beneath the cotton. He wanted to reach out and touch her, feel the tight buds under his fingertips, against his tongue. Averting his eyes, he focused on her face. "You need to shower."

She yawned. Her mouth gaped open in a full-bodied exhale—right into his face.

"And you need to brush your teeth. Wow." He chuckled, leaning back a few inches.

Her eyes sprang open while her mouth snapped shut. A hand slapped over her lips while the other gathered the edge of the blanket and pulled it up to her chin. "What are you doing in my room?" she asked, her voice muffled.

"Trying to wake you up." He hovered at the edge of her bed, awestruck by how amazing she looked while still half asleep. He didn't usually stick around long enough to see women in bed in the morning, but he liked what lay in front of him—messy hair splayed out on the pillow, eyes heavy with lingering dreams, curves barely concealed by pajamas.

All good.

"What time is it?" she mumbled.

"You've got twenty minutes."

"Twenty minutes?" she squeaked, bolting upright.

Throwing back the blankets, she sprang from the bed.

Sawyer rose beside her, taking in the landscape of her long legs, slim waist, and perky breasts along the way.

"My head." She moaned and swayed on her feet. Instinctively, he slipped an arm around her body to steady her.

"You might be a touch hung over. Hopefully a nice hot shower will help. While you're in there, I'll fix you a coffee and some breakfast. Eggs?"

She groaned again. "I might be sick."

"So no eggs then." He helped her walk to the bathroom, where she splashed cold water on her face.

Droplets fell from her chin as their eyes locked in the mirror's reflection. "I can't believe I did this."

"Don't worry about it. Everyone drinks too much sometimes."

"True. But does everyone go to their second day of work hung over?" She pressed her cheek to the granite-topped vanity, sighing. It didn't look like the most comfortable position to be in, although it wasn't bad for an observer. "I suck at this whole working thing. I should go back to being a nomad, where I rarely made an ass of myself."

At her reference, his gaze darted below her waist. Her ass looked pretty damn good in those little shorts. "You have no reason to be embarrassed."

"Really? Day one, I basically see my boss naked. Day two, I'm hung over. Very professional."

He laughed. "I happen to have it on good authority, your boss is a nice guy who may or may not have forgotten to lock the bathroom door before getting naked, therefore he's taking partial blame for the incident. And rumor has it he even once showed up to work so hung over, he might have actually still been a little inebriated. I'm sure he'll cut you some slack."

She smiled weakly, squinting and rubbing her forehead. "Maybe the boss guy also has a hangover cure? Or a few pain relievers?"

"Done and done. Shower. I'll bring you everything."

While he waited for the coffee to brew, he scrolled through his schedule for the day: back-to-back meetings, as usual. Clicking to his monthly calendar, he checked any notations for the upcoming weeks. One caught his eye immediately—the gala.

The gala he attended every year was rolling around again. Dread filled him at the thought of going to yet another one alone. Every year he went because it was a good opportunity to work on his client relationships, and maybe even forge a few new ones. And every year, halfway through the night, he wished for an excuse to leave. It would be way more fun if he had someone with him—someone who always seemed to have fun, no matter what the situation.

Olivia would be the perfect date. Not only did he like her company, she might also enjoy a fancy night out. He couldn't imagine she'd had many opportunities for those in the last few years while she traveled. They usually had a good band and delicious food.

He'd give anything not to attend, but this year it was more important than ever to be there. Cultivating and maintaining his clients was a priority if he wanted Sterling Enterprises to be around next year.

Olivia would probably do well networking for her next job while they were there, too. He'd seen how quickly she'd won over his family and the people at work. She'd have no problem schmoozing with possible contacts for an evening. Hell, if she used any of that natural charisma on his clients, half of his worries would be over. At least with her by his side for the night, he had a hope of enjoying it this year. Now he just needed to convince her to join him.

He filled a mug with coffee and wandered to the bathroom with his arsenal of hangover supplies. He found her at the vanity where he'd left her, only now she was dressed, her hair pulled back into a tight twist. "Take the pills with the water first, then work on the coffee."

With her first sip of coffee, she sighed and let her eyes flutter closed. When she opened them again, she smiled. "You are the best boss ever. Next time you need something at work, I'm your girl."

He liked the sound of that. "Actually, there's this fancy, sort of stuffy, yet kind of over the top gala that I go to every year. The food is usually pretty good and the band is decent. I'd like it if you would be my date for the evening."

"Well, when you sell it like that, how could a girl refuse?" She laughed then cringed as if her head ached. "When is it?"

"Two weeks."

"Will anyone who needs to believe our scam be there?" she asked, sweeping mascara along her lashes.

"I have no idea, but if anyone gets word that our relationship isn't real, it could travel back to my family. It wasn't that long ago that my grandfather ran the business. For all I know, some of his old buddies will be there. I thought it'd be a good way for you to start networking, too. There are usually a lot of big name CEOs attending. Never know where you'll meet your next boss."

The thought of her working for someone else settled

like a lead brick in his stomach. He'd only worked with her for one day so far, but he liked having her at the office. She brought a certain quality to the atmosphere that hadn't been there before. It was hard to describe in words. It was more of a feeling, like a bolt of lightning had hit his building and Sterling Enterprises was suddenly electrified with new energy.

She rubbed her temples then took another sip of coffee. "Okay. Sure."

"Great. You'll probably need a new dress, since I can't imagine you would've had room in your backpack for one. You can use my company credit card when you're ready to shop, and I'll bill it as a business expense."

"Gotta love free clothes. I'll probably need jewelry, too."

He smirked, happy to see her sense of humor returning. "I'm sure you'll find beautiful accessories. One more thing. It's out of town, so you'll need to pack an overnight bag."

Her mouth dropped open into an O-shape and her eyes met his in the reflection. *Yep, that was an important detail.*

His breath caught in his throat. *Don't say no.* The thought of going alone was even more unappealing now that he'd imagined taking her.

"Okay."

"Great!" His response was louder than he expected and he quickly cleared his throat, hoping she hadn't noticed how desperate he sounded. He realized with a mix of trepidation and anticipation, a weekend away with Olivia sounded better than he thought it would.

Chapter Eight

Olivia swallowed nervously. She had no reason to be nervous—it was only soccer practice—but even if her brain knew that, her body refused to listen. This was the first time she had to pose as Sawyer's girlfriend around his friends.

With his family and work, at least she knew their relationship and affection toward each other would be pretty conservative. But here, with his closest friends, she didn't know what to expect. Were they the "grab their girlfriend's ass in public" kind? The "compare sex stories" kind?

The thought of having to participate in a conversation about her and Sawyer doing it, made her heart pound. Fictional or real, sex with him made her knees weak.

"Why is your palm so sweaty?" he asked, taking her hand in his as they walked into Chelsea Piers.

Of course that's the thing he notices. Not the laid back yet put together outfit that took her almost an hour to achieve.

Nope. That was overlooked.

How could she say she was nervous about what she might have to talk about while hanging out? That sounded ridiculous. She sighed. "I'm nervous about meeting your friends."

She tried to take her hand back so she could wipe her palm on her pants leg, but Sawyer held strong.

"You have nothing to worry about. It's just a few guys running around a field after a ball. Actually, I think you'll like hanging out with the other women. They're all pretty nice. At least they seem nice. I haven't hung out with them that much, since I never have anyone on the sidelines watching me."

"What, you've never socialized with other girlfriends? I knew you were a lifelong bachelor, but that seems a little extreme, even for you."

"I've hung out with them after practice or a game, sure, but I've never had a girlfriend sit on the sidelines watching. I don't do the girlfriend thing. No need to be snippy."

"I wasn't being snippy. I was teasing." Olivia was halfway through a satisfying eye roll when she stopped herself. "How many more of these 'I'm annoyed with you' couple's spats are we going to have? If this were a real relationship, I'd say we're mildly toxic together."

He stopped and faced her. "Listen, I'm probably more uncomfortable than you are. This is huge for me. Gigantic. I don't bring girls here because I don't usually care enough about any of them to bother."

"Wow. I would probably feel special after that little admission if I didn't know the real reason I'm here. No worries. If anyone asks why you're off your game today, I'll tell them it's because I kept you up too late last night, fooling around." She tried to laugh it off, but sounded as fake as their relationship.

He opened his mouth as if to say something, but closed it again without speaking, then led her into the building and directly to the soccer field. A group of guys were already huddled together, while a cluster of girls sat off to the side, drinking iced coffees.

The women eyed Olivia as she walked up with Sawyer. "Hi, ladies. This is Olivia, my girlfriend."

She didn't miss the obvious expressions of disbelief. He hadn't been kidding about never bringing a girl around before. The knowledge that she was the first sent a little flash of pride through her.

"Hi," she said with a tiny wave.

"Get your ass out here!" Aidan called from the field.

"Olivia, this is Nina, Stacy, Kennedy, and April. I gotta go. Be nice to my girl." He pointed at the women as if he were scolding them, and then gave her a quick kiss on the cheek before jogging out to join the guys.

She wasn't sure what shocked her more, the quick kiss or that he'd called her "his girl" with a genuinely possessive tone. Feeling a little stunned, she smiled and sat down with the women.

"Girlfriend?" Stacy tilted her head inquisitively.

"Yep. That's me." She tried to channel her inner cool girl, who wouldn't be fazed by meeting new people. Apparently, that girl slept in this morning. "Which guy out there is yours?"

"Chad and I are newlyweds. Nina is with Jason. April just started dating Kevin. And Kennedy is with TJ, this week at least."

"I have trouble picking one," Kennedy said, with a

wicked smile playing on her lips. "They're all so hot when they get sweaty."

She didn't know how to respond. The thought of Kennedy and Sawyer fooling around instantly set her nerves on edge.

"Don't worry, she hasn't gotten to Sawyer." Stacy laughed and patted Olivia on the shoulder.

"Yet," Kennedy said, eyeing the guys on the field and making little noises in her throat as if the other girls weren't around to hear.

"Kennedy! Be nice. You're going to scare her off." April shook her head. "Really, you'd think the girl was sex-starved or something, which she's not."

"Glad to hear it?" Olivia said, not sure if she found their banter funny or problematic. "I guess I should start coming every week if I want to hold onto my man, huh?" She hoped her tone was teasing and playful. It felt strange to joke around with girls again. This wasn't something she'd done much of while backpacking.

"If you're not coming, that could definitely be a problem for you, and doesn't say much about Sawyer's skills either."

"Kennedy!" both Nina and April shrieked.

Olivia's cheeks burned and she giggled uncomfortably. This was exactly what she was afraid of. Bedroom talk. But she'd never guessed it would be the women who initiated the conversation.

As if he knew she was talking about him, Sawyer caught her eye and smiled, his arm flexing as he waved. He filled out his soccer shirt well. Really well.

"We have to tease a little since Sawyer's never had a girlfriend here before," Stacy said.

"Ever," Kennedy added.

April nodded enthusiastically. "It's a little weird, to be honest."

Either she would fit in right away, or not at all, and if she had to sit there with these girls on a regular basis, then she may as well do everything she could to be accepted by them, starting with breaking the ice about the whole girl-friend thing. The sooner they all got over that issue, the better. "I guess I took his relationship virginity, huh? He's doing pretty well, for a first-timer."

The girls sat stunned for a millisecond then burst out laughing so loudly the guys on the field turned to stare.

As conversation continued on to other, non-Sawyer-related topics, Olivia relaxed. She seemed to fit in with the dynamic of the group easily, chiming in with stories about her travel. Before she knew it, she felt as if she'd been friends with these girls for months, not minutes.

Maybe she shouldn't have been so nervous. If she had to do this more often, maybe it wouldn't be such a terrible thing after all. First his family had accepted her, and now his friends. Fitting into Sawyer's life was easier than she'd expected. But was that good or bad, when she knew that these real friendships she formed would all be gone when her fake relationship expired?

•••

Sawyer kicked at the ball as it rolled past him, but he underestimated its speed and missed, gloriously. He almost lost his balance as his leg flung out spastically. "Damn it." He'd been playing like shit all practice long.

Normally he was solid on the field. No matter what else was going on in life or at work, when he ran out to play, he was focused and determined to win. But it wasn't every day he had Olivia on the sidelines watching him either. Today he was sloppy and distracted.

It started when he'd seen and heard the girls laughing. He'd glanced over to see if Olivia was laughing with them or if they were laughing at her. Thankfully, even from across the field, he'd been able to see the smile on her lips. But then, instead of going back to focusing on drills, he started thinking about how great it was to see her getting along with the other women. She'd been clearly nervous that morning, but he knew she'd be fine and fit in with everyone.

"Let's take five before we do our scrimmage," Jason said, as he turned to trot off the field. As team captain, it was up to him to call the breaks. Sawyer was happy not to have the extra responsibility. He had enough stuff to think about without adding soccer to the list. On the field, he got to relax and enjoy the sport for the fun of it.

When he jogged over to the bench on the sidelines, Olivia handed him a fresh cold bottle of water and a granola bar, scooting over on the bench to make room for him beside her. It was nice having her there, doing girlfriend-type things. He'd seen it many times before, but had never been on the receiving end. He'd have to be careful not to get too used to this.

He leaned forward with his elbows on his knees and looked around at his buddies. They were all touching their girlfriends in some way. A hand on a knee, an arm around shoulders. A sudden wave of stupidity washed over him. Why was it so unnatural for him to treat her like a girlfriend should be treated? Because he sucked at being a boyfriend.

Shaking off the feelings of inadequacy, he leaned back and rubbed his hand up and down Olivia's spine. As soon as he made contact with her body, calmness passed through him. His heart rate slowed and a smile came to his lips.

She turned and grinned at him. "You're amazing out there."

"What about me?" Aidan asked, nudging his sister in the side.

"You're fine, too," she said, moving closer to Sawyer and a little farther from her brother's reach. He'd have to remember to thank Aidan later for that.

"Thanks," he said, enjoying her vote of confidence in his soccer skills. "I wish you could've seen me last week. I pretty much stink this week, comparatively."

"Yeah. What's up with you today?" Aidan asked. "You couldn't hit the ball if it was attached to your foot."

"I haven't seen you play this bad since…" Chad paused, tapping his fingers on his chin. "Since ever."

"I don't know. I'm tired I guess," he said. There was no other reason he could give them. He certainly couldn't tell them he was distracted because he kept thinking about his fake girlfriend.

"Here I thought you'd be eager to show off for your girl," Jason said.

"Guess you're not good at performing under pressure." Chad laughed. "Your poor girlfriend."

The guys laughed, except for Aidan and Sawyer. It wasn't cool to bring up his sex life with Olivia, even if it was only fictional. "Watch it. I won't have you talking bad about me around my girl."

The guys cheered and nudged each other.

"Defensive Sawyer. This is new," Kevin said.

"And don't forget she's my sister," added Aidan.

Chad held up his hands defensively. "No offense intended, Olivia. I'm sure you're worth performing for."

The guys fell silent and Sawyer held his breath, praying she wouldn't be offended by the teasing. The guys were jokers, but their hearts were usually in the right place. Their minds, however, were often in the gutter.

"Oh, I am," she said with a wink over her shoulder at Sawyer. "And he hasn't had any trouble performing. Even his encore is top notch."

The guys all hollered again and slapped Sawyer on the shoulder as they headed back out to the field. He beamed with Olivia's praise, even if it wasn't based on firsthand knowledge. The fact that she could think fast on her feet, and wasn't afraid to stand up for herself, or him, was a super sexy quality.

The girls he'd dated in the past had always been a little light in the smarts department and now he wondered why he'd ever bothered with girls like that when strong, confident women like Olivia were so much more engaging. Every time he thought he'd seen all sides of her personality, she surprised him with something new and interesting. Somehow he knew he could be with her every day for ten years and always learn something new about her.

Taking that challenge was almost too tempting.

He leaned over and gave her a quick kiss on the cheek, then ran out to the field again. He felt more calm and focused on the game than he had before; he didn't have to worry about her. Whatever happened, she could hold her own without him.

A little twinge of guilt prickled along his spine. She was doing so much to help him out, not only with getting the cabin but also with the Marcus project, and all he was doing was taking. He needed to give something back to her, something that would help her as much as she was helping him, something that would show how much her support meant to him.

Sawyer made a quick promise to himself that he would do whatever he could to make the gala a special night out for her, not only personally, but professionally, too.

Chapter Nine

Olivia stepped out of Sawyer's luxury SUV and smoothed her dress over her hips. She'd picked out a sleek crimson gown with a form-fitting silhouette and a side-slit up to the knee that made her feel taller and sexier than she actually was. Though she'd bought it off the rack, the dress looked as if it had been custom designed for her figure, hugging and caressing each curve like a lover's touch. The thought sent an image of Sawyer's hands to her mind and she swallowed hard.

The moment Sawyer first set eyes on her in the dress, his gaze raked over her, taking in every inch of the fabric and leaving behind a wake of electricity. When his eyes finally met hers again, a single word left his mouth. "Nice." A single word uttered, but his expression said enough for ten men.

She didn't want to care what he thought, yet at every opportunity, she found herself craving his praise. So far, he hadn't disappointed.

"Don't look so nervous." He handed the keys to the

valet and their small overnight bags to the bellman. When he offered his arm, she accepted. "You're not walking into your execution."

"I know. I don't want to make any mistakes that might cost you clients. What if I say the wrong thing?"

"You won't say the wrong thing." He sounded more confident than she felt.

"You probably should've brought someone else."

"First of all, you're my girlfriend, at least as far as everyone else is concerned. And secondly, even if you weren't my girlfriend, I can't think of anyone else I'd rather have with me. Certainly no one else would've filled out that dress the way you do." He clicked his tongue at the end of his sentence and raised an eyebrow suggestively.

"So I'm eye candy?"

"Yes and no. You're here because I'm stuck coming to this event every year, and this year I wanted to enjoy myself. I know I will with you. But I can't help it if you fit the eye candy description, too. I didn't tell you to wear that slinky little dress."

She'd never been anyone's shiny arm trinket before and she was relieved to know he saw her as more than that, not that she wasn't flattered by the suggestion. But she was the jeans and T-shirt, hair in a ponytail, let's go hiking type, not the put on a fancy dress and mingle type.

Passing through the lobby, she pointed out the front desk. "Shouldn't we check in?"

"Matt is already here and he checked in for us. I'll get the room key from him." He guided her toward the ballroom at the other end of the lobby.

Key? As in singular room but multiple beds, right?

"The concierge will make sure our room is ready by the time we head up for the night."

"And when will that be?" she asked.

"Are you sick of me already?" The twinkle in his eyes hinted at playfulness. She rarely got to see that side of him. Even at home, his home, he was usually thinking about work, or his grandparents, or both. The only time she'd seen him let loose was the few occasions they'd hung out with her brother or while the guys were playing soccer. Seeing this other part of his personality always made her want to smile, relax, and have fun too.

"Of course not. I was only curious how late this gala usually goes. I won't turn into a pumpkin at midnight."

"I'm glad to hear that. I quite like you in your current form." Something about the way he said it made her wonder if there was truth to his teasing this time. "Now, are you ready to do some networking?"

"Why? Have you spotted one of your clients already?"

"No. But I see Lois Hanover, who I happen to be good friends with, over by the bar, and she might be someone you'd be interested in applying to in a few months. I'd like to introduce you."

"Really? I thought we were here for your work," she said. Was she ready to meet potential bosses? Not necessarily. However, if they were anything like Sawyer, then working with them could be great. Her nervousness shifted to excitement.

Maybe she *was* ready for this. Hadn't she been waiting for a chance to take charge of her future? And now Sawyer wanted to give her that opportunity through one of his connections. Just when she thought she had him pegged as kind of self-centered, he went and did something completely selfless, and at an event that was very important to his company's success, too.

"Don't be nervous. She's going to love you as much as I do." His smiled wavered.

Her breath caught in her throat and she locked her eyes on his.

"Work wise, I mean," he added quickly.

"Of course. I didn't think you meant it in any other way." She nodded. Regardless of his slip of the tongue—which obviously didn't mean anything—she felt more confident in herself knowing he believed she'd impress Lois. She plastered a smile on her lips and squared her shoulders. "Lead the way."

For the first hour, Olivia was introduced to various people—some clients, some Sterling executives she hadn't met yet, and many possible future employers. She smiled, nodded, and laughed when appropriate. She lost track of the number of times she spoke about her education and travel. Sawyer guided her through the room, whispering tidbits of information along the way so she had an idea who each person was. Together they fell into an almost choreographed tag team, each talking up the other's attributes in a way that came off as conversational instead of forced.

She hadn't felt this exhilarated in a long time. Maybe never. Sawyer made a great professional wingman and she hoped she'd done the same. By the time they stopped mingling long enough to enjoy sipping a glass of wine, she realized she hadn't fully appreciated the grandeur of the venue.

The ballroom was adorned with ornate crystal chandeliers, rich cream and gold paint, and gleaming hardwood floors throughout. In the center of the room, surrounded by tables, a large area was filled with couples dancing. The live band seamlessly flowed between up-tempo and slow songs. Currently, they were on an upswing and it helped give the room a festive, celebratory feeling.

She eyed the dance floor tentatively. She wanted to enjoy the music, and she would, as long as he didn't ask her to dance. When it came to dancing, she had two left feet and neither one of them had an ounce of rhythm.

"What's wrong?" he asked, whispering into her ear.

She turned her head slightly to look at him, but also to get his lips away from her ear. What she really wanted to do was lean into him, cocoon herself in his arms, and let his breath play on her body at its will. But she damn well wasn't going to let that happen. "Nothing," she replied. "Why?"

"You look upset. Or concerned about something suddenly."

"I'm not."

"You are. I can see it all over your face."

Sighing, she answered honestly, against her better judgment. "I don't like dancing."

"All women like to dance."

"Not this one." Couples twirled and dipped, laughed and smiled, while shimmying to the music. Dread sank in her stomach like an anchor. "That part isn't mandatory, right?"

He smiled. "You're lucky I'm in a generous mood. I won't make you dance with me, even though I really want to see how terrible you are."

"Nice. So my humiliation is your entertainment?"

He kissed her cheek before whispering in her ear again. "I won't make you do anything you don't want to. Not here.

Not ever."

Was he still talking about dancing?

"Let's go find some food."

"It smells delicious. They certainly know how to throw a party." Olivia took a plate and meandered past the buffet. Everything from simple sliced vegetables and dip, to oysters on the half shell, pastas…even a selection of caviar was displayed.

No sooner had they sat to eat when Sawyer quickly wiped his mouth and hands, took a swig of his drink and cleared his throat. He stood from the table and extended his hand.

"What a pleasant surprise to see you here," Sawyer said, shaking hands with a tall, dark-haired man who looked imposing and serious, even with a smile on his face.

"It was a last minute thing. We were supposed to be out of the country, but last night our plans changed, so here we are. It's nice to see you make it out of the office on occasion." The man chuckled and smacked him on the shoulder, then gestured to the woman beside him. "This is my wife Ruth."

"It's nice to meet you." He shook her hand. "This is Olivia."

She stood, fighting the urge to check her teeth for little bits of food. Instead she smiled with her lips closed and shook the hand offered. "It's nice to meet you."

"You must be Sawyer's wife," the man said.

She held her smile while trying to glance casually to Sawyer, unsure of how he would handle the wife comment. Better than expected, it appeared. He wrapped his arm around her waist and pulled her close, his hand low on her hip, almost possessively.

"Olivia is my girlfriend. For now at least, right, sugar?"

She smiled adoringly at him. Not knowing who they were playing this up to, she did her best to look convincing.

The man kissed the back of her hand like a southern gentleman would. "Don't wait too long. You wouldn't want someone else to come and snatch her away. When I met my Ruthie, I was smitten at first glance, but had an ego too big for my head. So I dragged my feet and some other fella nearly swept her up. I learned my lesson back then, not to wait on things I want. Applies to work too."

"What kind of work do you do?" Olivia asked, smiling politely. He seemed quite nice and not nearly as imposing as she thought at first glance.

"This is Todd Marcus," Sawyer said.

"Oh." She swallowed her sudden unease. This was their most important client and now she'd gone and not even recognized him.

Todd raised his eyebrows questioningly at her obvious shift to nervousness. Sawyer was right—people could read her emotions on her face. She'd make a terrible double agent. Hopefully she could manage to keep their fake relationship a secret.

"I see someone's been bringing their work home to the little lady, huh?" Todd asked, but she couldn't tell if he was upset about the idea or kidding around.

"Actually, Olivia also works at Sterling. She's an essential part of our team."

"Oh?" Now he was the one who sounded surprised and caught off guard. "And what exactly do you bring to the team?"

"I'm an administrative assistant mostly, but I have been

trying to help out where I can with your project."

"Life experience. Cultural insights from around the world," Sawyer said, sounding almost a little defensive. "She is too modest. She's really the key to authenticity with your campaign. With her knowledge we'll be able to better target specific demographics in multiple countries."

"Sounds wonderful. I'd love to hear more about it. Care to dance?" Todd extended his arm and the dread in her stomach became full-fledged anxiety. Sawyer gave the slightest nod, his smile never faltering.

She allowed Todd to lead her out to the dance floor. A waltz-style rhythm filled the air. "I'll try not to step on your feet, but I must warn you that you've chosen a terrible partner."

"Not to worry," Todd said, gliding her around the dance floor with surprising ease. She almost felt as if she were floating. "I've had a terrible dance partner for the last twenty years. My feet no longer feel the stab of high heels."

Olivia stumbled, but quickly regained her footing. "Good thing."

"So tell me, how is it you have all this cultural insight and knowledge?"

"I backpacked around the world for a while. I guess that makes me something of an expert, or at least according to Sawyer it does."

"But not to you?"

Crap. How would Todd Marcus believe they could do a good job if she disputed everything Sawyer claimed? The fact was, she did have more cultural experience globally than anyone else in the Sterling office, so she was the resident expert. She needed to start believing it herself.

"Well, I wouldn't say I'm an expert, necessarily, but I do have experience with other cultures, which might be helpful in figuring out how we can make your product a staple in every home, in every market."

"And how exactly do you plan to do that?"

Shit. Good question. Think. I can totally do this.

"I would start by looking at what each culture values most and then base the marketing on that."

"Humor me with an example."

It was hard to think with the room continually spinning around them as they moved. From somewhere in her peripheral vision she saw Sawyer chatting and dancing with Ruth, looking carefree as if this was any other day to him. Meanwhile, her pulse drummed in her ears louder than the music.

She'd always done well in high-pressure situations. This was no different.

"Okay, let's say one region really values health more than anything else. Then we would focus the advertising on the whole person, and how your product can nourish them from the inside out. Healthy lives begin from the inside out and from the ground up."

"I like that 'ground up' part. I've been trying to come up with ways my company can leave a smaller carbon footprint while still reaching its goals. It's tough to pull off." Marcus twirled her around in time to the music.

"The problem as a whole is somewhat overwhelming, true, but the solution could be as simple as a tiny change. Take for instance the amount of plastic we use in this world. Huge, right? But if everyone switched to reusable bottles, even just for water, then think of how much less plastic would be tossed away. Maybe you need to break your issue down into a more manageable portion. Focus on one change for the better."

"I see your point. What other ways might we tailor our advertising?"

"In a region where they value family, maybe we would show how your products can seamlessly slip into their daily lives, making families healthier without getting in the way of all the other activities they do in a day. Big health, small package. Or you know, something like that."

She bit her lip and prayed she hadn't said anything stupid. Already, her words were gone from her memory. She'd always found it difficult to retain information when she was nervous.

"I like what I hear," Todd finally said, as the song stopped.

Instantly, Sawyer and Ruth were by their side.

"This one's a keeper. I think you're right about her. She's definitely an asset, and I hope you won't keep her hidden away next time I'm at the office. I'd like to hear more of her thoughts."

"Absolutely. As I said, she's an important part of our team."

"I look forward to talking with you again. Soon. Enjoy your evening."

The men shook hands and said pleasant goodbyes. Before she could object, Sawyer had her pulled in close, his hands on her lower back, his hips swaying to the slow, sensual beat of the music.

"You promised me no dancing," she said, peering up at him. It wasn't her favorite thing, but being in his arms certainly made the experience more tolerable. *This* she could get on board with.

"I didn't know Todd would ask you, but I'm glad you agreed. What did you talk about? He seemed smitten with you."

Was that a hint of jealousy in his tone?

"He wanted to know what made me an expert. I have no idea what I said to him. I hope it wasn't something way off the mark."

"Seemed like he dug your ideas, whatever they were. We'll have to go over the conversation later, when you're less distracted."

He grinned down at her. The spark of fire she often saw at work was in his eyes, full-force, but there was something else, too. Excitement? Intensity?

"I really did bring you here because I wanted to enjoy the evening with you. I had no idea you'd be helping me win over my clients as well. You're amazing."

She shrugged, her cheeks warming with his praise. "I try."

"Funny thing is, I don't think you even have to. You're a natural at this stuff."

"When I was away, if I didn't make conversations with strangers, I wouldn't talk to anyone. It didn't take long to learn I needed communication or I'd go crazy."

His hand pressed against her lower back more firmly, forcing her body to make contact with his. The thin material of her dress did nothing to protect her from the feel of his body rubbing along hers, awakening it in ways she enjoyed more than she cared to admit. Every time he was near, she felt as if she'd woken from a long sleep.

Slipping her arms around his shoulders to cuddle deeper

into his embrace, she fingered the cropped hair behind his ears. His eyelids dropped as her fingertips stroked the nape of his neck. All the swaying, slow music, and body heat made her wish for when this part was over so she could slip out of her dress, into pajamas, and what she hoped was a luxuriously soft bed. The thought made her sigh with contentment.

The song ended and she stopped moving, but the pause was only momentary before achingly long, drawn out notes began to play again. Deep, crooning vocals seeped from the speakers. Thick, rolling waves of sexual undertones washed over her.

Their bodies swayed together while her hands traced the lines of his shoulders and chest, exploring his form as much as possible while still in the company of others. She was powerless to stop herself. No, not powerless. She didn't want to stop. Being in his arms felt too good. She wanted to know what the rest of him felt like. As if hearing her thoughts, he tilted her chin up to him as if he was thinking about kissing her. His thumb brushed across her bottom lip, his eyes dipping slightly as he examined her.

Kiss me already.

No longer caring about what was right or wrong for their pretend relationship, she simply wanted him to kiss her. She'd been fantasizing about another kiss since the first one at the family dinner.

Opening her mouth the tiniest bit, she ran her tongue along the edge of her teeth, an invitation only he would see. And he did. The hand still heating her lower back increased the pressure on her skin.

Her breath caught with anticipation as his gaze darted around the room. When his eyes settled on her again, he pressed his lips to hers gently. She waited to feel his lips open over hers like they had last time. Instead, it was as if he wanted more, but was holding back. She felt like a pot of water on the verge of boiling.

"Get a room," a man teased over the loud music.

Sawyer gave her one last little peck on the lips. When she finally pried her eyes away from his face, where she was desperately trying to read his expression, she found Matt dancing with his wife, a goofy grin on his face.

"It's not often I see you in a lip lock. Hell, never. It's odd. And disgusting. Really, you two should get a room if you can't keep your hands off each other long enough to socialize."

"How could I resist kissing a woman as beautiful as Olivia? Besides which, that was just a peck. If you think that was a real kiss, I may need to give you lessons, to save your poor wife from a lifetime of misery."

Olivia didn't miss Sawyer's playful wink. Not a real kiss? Did he mean that, or was he teasing his friend?

"Don't worry about us. We'll make good use of our room later." His wife smacked him playfully on the arm while he flipped a plastic key card out of his pocket. "Oh, and look what I have here."

"Thanks," Sawyer said, pocketing the key card. "We got away from the city later than I wanted."

"No problem. Are you enjoying yourself tonight, Olivia? Sawyer hasn't been talking about work the whole time, has he?" Matt asked.

"It's been wonderful. A good mix of work and play. Actually, a bunch of the work talk has been networking on my behalf."

"You're not thinking about leaving us already, are you? You've been a great addition to the team."

"It's a term position. I have to think about what's next sometime, right?" she asked. "I have really been enjoying my time at Sterling so far, though."

With Sterling, too. Sawyer Sterling.

"Maybe we'll have to think about giving her a permanent position before we lose her to the competition."

"You might be right," Sawyer said, holding her tight. "I might not be able to let her go."

His warm lips pressed against her cheek and she melted into his embrace, overwhelmed by how much she wanted to feel his body connecting to hers.

"Now seriously, either keep it clean or move the public displays of affection to somewhere a little less public. There must be a coat room around, if you need to get it out of your system." Matt laughed.

"Matt!" his wife squeaked. "Honestly, you men are all disgusting. All you think about is sex."

"Yeah. And?" Matt and Sawyer said at the same time, before laughing.

Olivia rolled her eyes along with Matt's wife, even though she didn't feel at all like joking. The thought of Sawyer taking her to a coat closet to have his way with her made her knees turn to liquid and her panties suddenly dampen.

"We'll be good for the rest of the night. Scout's honor." He held up his hand as if taking an oath.

"I think that only means something if you're ten," Matt shot back.

Sawyer shrugged. "I was never a scout anyway."

Both men laughed again, then Sawyer took her hand

and led her off the dance floor. "Matt definitely bought it."

"Bought what?" she asked.

"The kiss. The flirting. I saw him coming and figured it was as good a time as any to convince him we're the real deal. I can't exactly kiss you at work."

"I thought it was only your family we were trying to fool." Why had he made it feel so real?

His gaze held hers but she couldn't read his expression— shocked, guilty, lying…aroused, wanton—she saw a lot in his eyes tonight. Too much.

She cursed silently. Which was she supposed to believe? What she felt or what he told her?

"I can't let it slip to anyone that we're not really a couple. Gramps still has too many connections to the Sterling Enterprises world." He said it in a way that made her feel like he was trying to convince himself as much as her. His expression softened. "Maybe I had a little too much to drink tonight and misread the situation. I only meant to solidify our relationship in Matt's eyes. That's all."

Of course his kiss wasn't a lead-in to something more. He was only ensuring their story looked real with the least amount of actual contact between them—exactly what she *should* want him to do.

Her heart sank. The heat in his kiss was nothing more than wishful thinking. Once again, she'd let her overactive imagination make her believe in emotions that didn't exist. She needed to accept that his feelings for her were nothing more than an act. Period. He'd told her himself he didn't want anything more than a fake relationship, and from now on she needed to remember that.

They made their way to the bar, got a drink, and circulated

the room, stopping every few feet to talk to another client or potential client. She was glad for the interaction with people. It distracted her from her own thoughts about how silly she was for falling for Sawyer's kiss again. How many times would he kiss her before it didn't affect her? If he could play along with their scam without getting caught up in the moment, why couldn't she?

By the time they'd made a few loops around the room, the crowd had thinned out, dagger-like pain shot through her feet, and she feared her smiling muscles might be permanently stuck in position. The entire time, Sawyer hadn't stopped touching her. Usually his arm was around her waist, his hand on her hip. Occasionally, they would lace their arms together between them. Sometimes he would simply hold her hand. But every minute, there'd been contact. And every minute, she'd fought with herself about wanting more from him—even while knowing it was absolutely, without a doubt, the exact wrong thing for her to want. She shouldn't want to be with Sawyer in any other way than professionally, yet she couldn't stop herself from aching for him with a need so deep and all encompassing that it made her head spin.

"I don't know about you, but I'm ready to call it a night." He covered a yawn with his hand and looked around the room. She didn't see anyone they hadn't already spoken to.

"I'm ready." Her gaze fluttered up to his, meeting it only for a moment before she glanced away again. Her throat felt tight with nerves.

She was about to spend the night in the same room as Sawyer. Would she be able to ignore the spark between them that threatened to catch fire every time they touched? Was she really the only one who felt it?

The elevator ride was silent except for the chanting in her mind: *Tonight will be fine... Tonight will be fine...*

He pushed open the door to their hotel room and she walked in. A king-sized bed took up most of the space. Both of their bags lay on the top of the dresser. A small table filled the corner. The only other door was the one leading to the bathroom, not another bedroom as she'd initially hoped... not another bed to make resisting him a tiny bit easier.

One room.

One bed.

And Sawyer.

Chapter Ten

One room.

One bed.

And Olivia.

Shit.

"This looks nice." Sawyer strode into the room as if he hadn't a care in the world—the exact opposite of the turmoil currently churning up the inside of his body. He'd spent the entire evening touching Olivia. Every second made him imagine being with her more, had tempted his body and mind, had made him ache with need.

What he really needed now was space away from Olivia.

"Sure. This is great. Cozy." She wrapped her arms across her chest. The position pushed her breasts together, swelling her cleavage in the deep neckline of her dress to the point he thought it might overflow.

I could get cozy here with those breasts... Can't let that happen.

Maybe he needed a soapy hand in the shower later, but he was okay with that if it meant keeping his cool where she was concerned.

Hell, he hadn't had anything beyond kisses from her since this whole charade started. No going to the bars to relax, drink, and pick up chicks. No grinding on the dance floor, making out in taxis, or quickies. Nothing but a couple of random kisses and touches from Olivia. But those kisses had been more than enough to make his balls tight and his dick hard. He needed a release soon or he might die. Death by blue balls sounded painful.

"So, one bed, huh?" Olivia asked.

"I'll call the front desk and see if I can get us a different room."

She surveyed the room for a moment before nodding and excusing herself to go to the bathroom. As soon as she disappeared behind the closed door and he heard the water running in the sink, he let out a long sigh. They needed a second room, or at the very least a second bed.

By the time she was out of the bathroom—hair down and a little wild, makeup washed off, but still in her beautiful dress—he was off the phone.

"The hotel is booked solid. The only other room available is the penthouse. I didn't book it, but if you want me too, I will."

She sighed. "No. I can't imagine how much that would cost. It's only one night. I'm sure we can manage."

"I'll sleep on the floor and you can have the bed," he said without hesitation. By the window, next to the table and chairs, he'd have enough room to curl up with a blanket and pillow.

"Chivalrous of you, but no. It's a king. There's plenty of room for both of us." She opened her bag and pulled out a tank and matching shorts. Not that he was paying attention or anything. "I'll go change."

Slipping out of his jacket and tie, he draped them across the back of a chair. He was unbuttoning his shirt when the bathroom door opened again. While Olivia took him in, he stood frozen. When they finally locked gazes, there was fire in her eyes and his exposed flesh felt as if it had been scorched.

She hesitated in the doorway before stepping toward him. "My zipper is stuck."

He met her near the foot of the bed. She turned her back, but not before her gaze had a chance to rake across his chest again. His heart pounded against his ribs as he reached for her.

"Your hair is in the way," he said, sweeping it over her shoulder.

"Sorry." She sounded almost breathless.

Her skin was soft as he ran his hands down her spine to the edge of her dress. She trembled under his fingertips, and her breathing hitched in her lungs.

"Relax, sugar. This will only take me a second. You've gotten the material all bunched up in the teeth," he said, gently pulling. He could think of a few ways he'd like to have the material of her dress all bunched up in his teeth. Lucky zipper.

Sawyer wiggled the zipper up and down while trying to slip the extra material out of the way. Finally, the silky fabric slipped to the side and the zipper moved freely and quickly. As it did, his knuckles skimmed along her skin, all the way to the curve of her lower back. With a struggling intake of breath, he noted her distinct lack of undergarments.

"You've been commando all night?" he whispered, disbelieving. *Goddamn.* Gripping her waist in both hands, he fought for control. His dick strained painfully against his boxer briefs. Air caught in his lungs, making it hard to clear his head of the lust-filled fog suddenly taking up residence between his ears.

Closing his eyes, he tried to force the sight of her from his mind, but couldn't. Her bare back brushed against his naked chest, leaving a tingle of electricity. The soft curves of her ass rubbed against his growing erection as she twisted slightly. Closing his eyes hadn't blocked out anything. Instead it had intensified his other senses.

His grip on her waist tightened. A deep inhale only assaulted him with the fragrance of warm vanilla and some kind of spice. Olivia smelled good enough to eat, and if their first kiss was any indication, she tasted even better. Or at least her mouth did. He could only imagine what the rest of her might taste like.

He wanted to find out. Now.

She peeked over her shoulder, her arms folded across her chest, holding her dress in place — the only thing standing between him and her completely naked body. One quick tug and that beautiful dress could be on the floor.

"I think I can manage from here. Thanks," she said quietly. Her eyes were clear and bright, not a hint of intoxication after the long night socializing.

Good. Then any decision she made tonight would be her own.

"Are you sure there isn't something else I can help you

take off?" He flattened his palm on her lower abdomen, his fingers wandering dangerously close to inappropriate places. What he wouldn't give to dip his hand lower, feel her heat through the thin material. He didn't need to ask if there was more to remove. They both knew what she wore under that dress. Nothing.

She turned in his arms, still holding her dress to her chest. "We can't do this."

"Do what exactly?"

"This. Whatever you're hinting at. We can't."

"I thought I was being obvious, not hinting. But regardless, we can." *And I want to,* he added silently.

"We made an agreement to keep things platonic."

"I've decided that was stupid." She was right, of course, but he didn't want to tell her that. If he were smart, he'd turn around and walk out of the room right now, go down to the front desk and get the key to the penthouse suite. Money well spent for a man in his predicament.

If he crossed this line with Olivia, there was a good chance his friendship with Aidan would be strained or blown to pieces completely. Could he risk a lifetime of friendship for a night of passion?

If that night was spent with the woman who'd held his mind and body captive in a perpetual purgatory of desire, need, and denial? Aidan would understand, given enough time.

Or he'd buy him beers until he forgot.

No. I gave my word.

That voice in his head reared up again. He should resist, walk away, run away if he had to. Too much was at stake. If he didn't, she might leave, call their agreement null and void.

He needed her to secure the cabin, his future…the place he felt closest to the memory of his parents. If his cousin succeeded in getting the cabin, Sawyer would have nowhere to call home. But he couldn't seem to convince his dick to listen. Hard to the point of painful, his body demanded her, holding his rational thoughts hostage for the ransom she could only pay with her body, her tongue.

"We did promise ourselves, and each other, you're right," he said, sighing. His fingers threaded through her hair, his thumbs tilting her chin up to him. In his head, somewhere far off in the distance, he knew all the reasons why he shouldn't kiss her. But the second her lips parted, and her tongue flicked beyond her teeth while she found her voice—the smoldering spark of attraction he'd been feeling all evening, with every touch, flared to life inside him. Gone was the ability to resist her, replaced by a need so primal it overrode everything else.

Sawyer crushed his mouth to hers. She responded against him, her lips inviting him in. Any hesitation vanished as her body melted into his. She tasted like cranberry juice and vodka. He couldn't get enough of her flavor on his tongue. He could drink her up all night. He'd been imagining kissing her like this for too long. He'd barely kept himself in check on the dance floor earlier, but now, in privacy, she was finally in his arms, kissing him, her body molded to his, and he didn't want to stop. Not now, possibly not ever.

She shifted against him. The swell of her breasts pressed into him, only the thin, silky material preventing the flesh-on-flesh he craved so deeply. She tilted her head and kissed him even harder.

"I've wanted to do that all night. It killed me not to

really kiss you earlier, but now…" He paused, pulling back enough to look at her.

"So you lied earlier? Or you're lying now? Which is it?"

"What are you talking about?"

"That kiss earlier, you said it was only to convince Matt we're a couple, but now you're saying it was something more. So at one point you lied to me, and I want to know when. I deserve to know the truth if you think anything like this is going to happen between us."

His sighed, resting his forehead against hers and closing his eyes. "You're right. I lied. Earlier. I wanted to kiss you all night. I was looking for a good excuse and when I saw Matt coming, I jumped at the opportunity."

"So why didn't you say that afterward? Why make up a reason?"

"I made a deal not to want to kiss you, Olivia. I told you I'd keep things professional and now I want to kick myself because I'm forced to keep my end of the deal. No matter what we agreed to, I can't help the way you make me want to rip the clothes off your body practically every time I see you. You…do something to me. I can't take it anymore." He needed confirmation that she wanted it too, before moving further. He didn't want to risk any assumption. One little whispered "yes" and he'd have her naked on the bed in a heartbeat. "I want this. I want you."

She gasped, trying to catch her breath. "You want me now, but you won't tomorrow, or the next day, or the month after that. This is all temporary, these feelings, this arrangement, all of it. As much as I might want you in this moment, I can't. I won't."

He clenched his jaw at her reaction, willing his erection

to cease and desist so he could think clearly. It refused. Dropping his hands to her waist, he fought the desire to argue with her. Usually women became putty in his hands, letting him caress them, squeeze them, ravish them in any way he saw fit. Olivia was different. He'd known that all along, but her refusal to give in to something they both so clearly wanted was another example of how she was unlike any other woman he'd ever met. And it made him want her all the more.

"Why can't you give in to what you want?"

"Because every time I give in to even a touch, I feel… something, then you turn around and tell me it's all part of the act. How do I know this isn't all part of the act, too?"

He motioned toward his erection, noting how her expression changed as it pressed into her stomach. "This isn't fake. This is what you do to me." He tucked his head into her neck, breathing in her scent. He felt more intoxicated by her than he ever had by a night of binge drinking. "You drive me crazy and I can't get you out of my head. You're like a drug and I'm an addict. I need a hit."

She rubbed against him with a sigh that bordered on a moan of pleasure. Her desire was obvious. Her fingertips brushed across his nipple, escalating his desire. When she slid her hand down his abdomen to the waistband of his pants and played with the patch of crinkly hair at the edge of the material, he almost lost his cool completely. She tugged on his belt until his waist bumped her, and peered up at him through heavy-lidded eyes, with an expression that begged him to ravish her.

It was all the confirmation he needed. He took her hand and pressed it to his aching length. She circled his shaft and stroked him through his pants. His dick twitched with her touch, and he was unable to hold back a groan of satisfaction.

"This isn't going to change anything about our arrangement. It'll only make the next couple of months longer," she said matter-of-factly, while still stroking him, her eyes growing heavier by the second.

"You're right," he said, his breath coming out quicker with each movement of her hand. "But it also might make it more fun."

"If we do this…" She squeezed and he shivered with pleasure. "There's no going back. I wouldn't be another random hookup. You'll have to see me again. Every day. At home and at work. Are you really sure you can handle that?"

"I can if you can."

"My brother will kill you if he finds out."

"He'll kill both of us. But I don't plan to tell him. Do you?"

"Not a chance." Olivia stepped back, putting an inch of space between them, then dropped her arms to her sides. Her dress fell to a puddle of shimmering crimson around her ankles. "Sounds like we have another secret to hide."

The sight of Olivia standing naked before him was enough to make his knees weak and his pulse race. Her perky breasts saluted him with taut nipples he couldn't wait to suckle. Tan lines from a one-piece swimsuit preserved her ivory skin along her breasts and stomach as if the area was for his eyes only. He liked the thought of that.

He wrapped his hand around the nape of her neck and kissed her the way he'd been fantasizing about. Hard, needy, raw. It wasn't his best moment, but damn it, he was beyond the point of restraint. Now was about feeling—her hands on his body, his tongue on hers, himself plunged deep inside.

Turning with her in his arms, he pressed her back onto the bed then kissed a trail down her neck to her shoulders. Her nipples beaded as he rolled them in his fingers before dipping his head to suck one into his mouth. She groaned and arched her back. Exactly the response he craved. Her hands clawed at his shirt while leaving his dick aching for more attention.

Moving to the other breast, he bit down gently on her nipple, reveling in her gasp. He smiled against her skin, eager for her to enjoy what he could do other places.

Sitting back for a second, he took in the view of Olivia naked before him. Her knees were drawn together, hiding her most intimate area. Not for long.

Massaging her legs, he caressed the slope of her calves as they curved down to dainty ankles. She squirmed as his fingers brushed the underside of her foot.

"Ticklish?"

She nodded.

"Tempting," he smirked.

"Don't you dare," she said, trying to pull her foot out of his grasp. As she moved, he caught a glimpse of what waited for him farther north, and this time it was his own gasping intake of breath he heard.

He kissed her knee and she stopped fidgeting, moaning with pleasure. Her thighs parted slightly as she relaxed. He took it as an invitation and kissed a path up her inner thigh until he found her wet heat. His tongue flicked across her sensitive skin, making her grip the sheets while arching against his mouth. Her reaction to every stroke of his tongue made him eager to please her more. Her body trembled under his careful attention and she called out his name, urging him on. He had no desire to stop until she was fully satiated.

Hearing her pleasure made his dick even harder but he ignored his own needs. There'd be plenty of time to meet those later. Right now, he only wanted to focus on the sound of Olivia coming undone.

When she finally did, her nails raked across his shoulders as her thighs quivered around him. He'd never heard or felt anything as awesome as Olivia in the throes of ecstasy.

"That didn't tickle, did it?" He kissed her belly button, dipping his tongue inside. She moaned and squirmed. "How about here?"

"Stop. Enough." She tugged on his shoulders. He took his time, pausing to suckle each breast again.

He'd watched her walk around in tight skirts, thin pajamas, and sexy dresses for the last few weeks, fantasizing about how she would look, feel, and taste naked. Now that he finally had her that way, he was in no rush to finish the job.

By the time he'd made it the rest of the way up her body, she'd found her strength. She flipped him over onto his back and straddled his stomach, her heat radiating against the skin of his abdomen.

"You had your fun, now it's my turn," she said, bending to kiss him hard on the mouth. Her tongue swirled around his, mirroring his hunger. When she finally broke away, she slid down his body, taking his boxers with her.

"I'm pretty sure you had fun too, sugar. I definitely didn't hear any complaints."

She didn't waste any time exploring like he had. Her hot mouth wrapped around his length and it was like waking up in heaven. Every flick of her tongue was intensely arousing. Every stroke of her warm, wet mouth along his shaft amplified his desire to take her fully. By the time he made her stop, he could barely think straight.

"I need a condom," he said, holding on to his last rational thought.

"I didn't bring any." She sat back on her heels, leaving him exposed to the cold air. He ached to feel her heat surrounding him again.

"I did," he said, propping himself up on his elbows.

"Planned this, huh? And here I thought we were being spontaneous." She folded her arms across her chest, covering her breasts.

"Not planned," he groaned, pent up sexual energy beginning to irritate him. "Hoped for maybe, but not planned. I'm a guy. I pretty much always think sex might be an option."

"Where are they?" she asked.

"My bag. Side pocket." He enjoyed the view as she walked around the room naked. At the sound of a foil packet ripping, he held out his hand. Instead of giving him the condom, she carefully rolled it down his length. He'd never been more turned on by a single action.

"You really did learn a few things while you were away, didn't you?" he asked as she climbed on top of him again. Normally he liked to be the one in control, but having her hovering over him, waiting to take him, he was willing to give over the reins.

She bit her bottom lip, looking innocent and seductive at the same time. "I knew before I graduated high school. But it did get lonely traveling. Every now and then it was nice to have some company of the foreign relations variety.

Men in other countries are talented at more than speaking multiple languages."

Oh, he'd give her multiple *somethings*, all right, and he'd do it without speaking a fucking word. Challenge accepted.

He wouldn't stop until he showed her how talented a little "Made in the USA" could be. With that in mind, he held her hips, lowering her slowly until he completely filled her. She threw her head back and sighed, accepting all he had to offer. When he thrust deep, she moaned and rolled her hips in time with him. Every thrust was better than the last, urging him on.

When she started to slow her pace, he flipped her over onto her back and shoved a pillow underneath her, raising her hips off the mattress. She wrapped her legs around his waist and gazed up at him with lust-filled eyes as he moved within her all encompassing heat—faster, harder, deeper.

Everything stopped. There was no hotel checkout time, no drive home, no work on Monday morning, and certainly not another woman in the universe as captivating and enticing as the one currently surrounding his body in warmth.

As he coasted near the edge of oblivion, she trembled for the second time, caressing his length with aftershocks and shattering any last hold he had on control. She called his name and clung to him while he tumbled after her, collapsing on her chest. His satisfaction was complete, uninhibited… mind-blowing.

For the first time he could remember, the urge to get dressed and leave didn't even enter into his realm of consciousness. He could happily stay there, wrapped in Olivia, for hours.

Shit, he cursed internally. *So much for temporary.*

Chapter Eleven

Sex wouldn't change anything, remember? Yeah, right.

If that was true, then why was she currently hiding in her room instead of hanging out in the living room watching TV like usual?

Because he's out there.

And that would mean more small talk like on the way home from the hotel. Conversations about unimportant nonsense and nothing about how they'd seen each other naked. Or how they'd given each other the most incredible orgasms. And the orgasms had been un-fucking-believable. Why couldn't he have been bad in bed so she'd be less inclined to be with him again?

Because he's Sawyer, and he's not bad at anything.

The man had skills. He could have a master's degree in the art of foreplay.

She'd said that sex with him wouldn't change anything because that's what she really wanted to believe in the moment. She'd wanted an excuse to give in, to be with him like she'd been fantasizing about, but of course she'd known all along how ridiculous that really was. How could one night in his arms, being kissed by him, touched by him…

Oh God, what his mouth could do.

What was done was done. She had to figure out how to get through the rest of this arrangement without either wanting to climb into bed with him again or feeling completely uncomfortable around him. She didn't want things to be awkward. She wanted things to be fun and flirty. They could be, couldn't they?

Then get out there and be not awkward!

Whether she wanted to or not, she had a relationship with Sawyer to maintain, both as his fake girlfriend and as his real roommate and employee. She'd given in as if it was a quick fling without ramifications to their relationship. But there were ramifications, and ignoring them wouldn't make them cease to exist. The best she could do was act mature about the whole situation and assume that he'd do the same. Luckily, this was nothing like her last experience with dating her employer. No one would go around slandering her name and ruining her reputation. They were consenting adults who'd made a decision. A stupid decision, possibly.

She smoothed her hair then opened her door. No going back now. The living room had two choices for seats: the big comfy chair over in the corner, where she liked to curl up and read, but watching TV was terribly uncomfortable, or the small couch facing the TV, where Sawyer was lounging in his gym shorts and a tight fitted T-shirt. She chose the couch. That was where she would have sat last week, so that was where she had to sit this week. *See, nothing's changed.*

"Hey," he said, as she snuggled under the throw blanket from the back of the couch. "I thought maybe you'd gone to bed early."

"Nope. Still up. Just hanging out in my bedroom for a while."

"Everything okay?" he asked.

"Sure. Fine. Why wouldn't it be?"

He shrugged. "No reason, I guess." Sawyer reached into the bowl of popcorn that was often on the couch between them and grabbed a handful. His strong fingers clutched the kernels without breaking them, reminding her of how he'd grabbed her rear, tenderly and commanding at the same time, while he'd kissed her in places that had made her quake with aftershocks.

Popcorn. Focusing on something else for a little while would take her mind off of Sawyer and his talent. As she shoved a handful into her mouth—*why be lady-like for a guy I'm not trying to impress, right?*—the salty taste of popcorn assaulted her taste buds. Her thirst tripled, and it did nothing to help her forget their night together.

Chocolate, she thought, heading to the kitchen. What every girl needed after any bedroom activity. The first three cabinets she rooted through produced not even so much as a chocolate chip. "Is there any chocolate in here?" she called, still searching.

"There should be, on a shelf to the left of the fridge."

She moved to the cabinet in question and scrounged more. Cans of soup, bottles of sports drinks, a few boxes of mac and cheese, but no chocolate of any kind. "Any idea which one?"

"This one right here." He reached around her to retrieve

the milk chocolate bar hiding behind a bottle of salad dressing. Clearly, the man had no idea how to organize his cabinets.

His warm breath tickled her earlobe, but it was nothing compared to the heat of his lips pressed to her neck. When his tongue flicked across her skin, a wave of pleasure coursed through her body, making her limbs wobbly and weak with desire.

"Stop," she whispered, trying to make her voice stern and confident. The last thing she wanted him to do just then was stop, but she couldn't give in to him again. Giving in would lead to more, and more would eventually lead to her heartbreak when their arrangement ended.

He was a mistake, and she shouldn't have let herself get carried away by him last night, no matter how amazing their night together had been. Great sex did not change the fact that she wanted long-term and he wanted right now. Theirs was probably the perfect set up for him—a roommate-with-benefits situation with a built-in expiration date.

"You didn't want me to stop last night." He nipped at her skin with his teeth.

He was good. Good enough to make a nun burn her habit.

"We agreed it wouldn't change anything, or have you forgotten that part already?" She turned to face him. His broad chest loomed inches away, begging for her touch, while his arms, with palms flat on the counter top, pinned her in place on both sides. Not a single piece of him physically touched her, but a million nerve endings had awakened with his proximity.

"I haven't forgotten. Nothing has changed. I'm still

your fake boyfriend for the next couple of months. We still work together, still live together, still flirt together at family functions. The only difference now is that the flirting doesn't have to stop when we're alone."

She didn't respond. What could she say? Part of her really wanted to agree with him, but the other part saw the warning signs—the giant red flags of his past, and what she wanted for her future.

"I know things were a little weird today. I can tell you're not sure what to do or how to act. It's strange for me, too, but I don't think it has to be. I'm still the same guy I was two days ago. The only difference now is that you don't have to hold back during those moments of desire I've seen flaring in your eyes when you look at me."

He stroked a path from her ear to the round of her shoulder with the back of his fingers. She fought the urge to lean into him. Already her body responded to him like a spark from a match.

"You know, that first night when you walked in here in your tiny night shirt, with just a thong on?" he asked.

Heat flashed in her cheeks. How could she forget? She'd never been so embarrassed. "Mmm," she mumbled, unable to find a word befitting the moment.

"What I did to you last night, I've been thinking about doing since then. You're always on my mind, and judging by the way you look at me, like you are right now, I'm on your mind, too. So instead of suffering through the next few months, pretending we didn't see each other naked, pretending I didn't kiss every inch of your body, pretending you didn't get pleasure from every second of my lips on your flesh…why don't we enjoy ourselves as much as we can?"

A tempting offer, but not one she could accept. It was flattering that he wanted to be with her, that he thought about her as much as she'd been thinking about him, but everything he wanted was temporary.

She wanted forever.

If she slept with him again, she feared she'd end up wanting forever...*with Sawyer.*

It was one thing to agree to an arrangement that was mutually beneficial, but getting into his bed again, maybe even multiple times over the next couple of months, wouldn't benefit her in the end.

She ducked under his arm. "Last night was awesome." He smiled and moved toward her, but she pressed her palms to his chest, keeping distance between them. "But it won't happen again. So unless we're with your family or someone else we have to fool, don't expect me to participate in flirting, touching, or kissing of any kind. Got it?"

He crossed his arms, jaw set, eyes narrowed. "Got it," he replied flatly.

As much as she wanted an encore performance, she couldn't allow it to happen. Not with Sawyer. Not now. Not ever.

Not without forever.

Chapter Twelve

Olivia knocked on the office door and crossed her fingers that tonight would go well. Earlier, Marcus had called and requested another meeting the following week, and now Sawyer was determined to work as many hours as needed to prepare, even if it meant not leaving the office until ten each night.

"Come in," Sawyer called.

"Dinner's here," she said, trying to be cheerful instead of stressed. "I didn't know what you'd want so I got a little of everything. Egg rolls, fried rice, beef and broccoli..."

"Great. Thanks," he said, without looking up from his computer.

She put the bag on the table then fished out the individual containers, setting them aside until she found the ones she'd ordered for herself—moo shu chicken and green beans. Taking a seat at the small table, she waited impatiently. "Are you going to stop long enough to join me for dinner?"

He was truly a man on a mission. He'd been going strong on the Marcus project since the meeting went on the books, but even he needed a break to eat, hydrate, and rest.

"I thought we were going to eat later." He looked more than a little annoyed.

"You can keep working if you want to, but I'm eating now. It's late, I'm starving, and the food is hot. And delicious, I gotta say." She let out a sigh of pleasure. Hoisin and soy sauce, scallion and garlic, mixed together on her tongue.

"I guess work will have to wait." He sat down across from her and opened various containers, taking a few forkfuls from each.

"You know, it's okay to take a little time for yourself. You're allowed to eat," she said. Pushing a reusable bottle of water toward him, she added, "and drink."

He raised an eyebrow at her. "I eat. I drink."

"I know, but maybe not enough." She took another bite while her words hung in the air. His expression didn't look amused. "I sit outside of your office every day, and I see how much you work without taking a single second out of your day for yourself. Aside from getting a refill of coffee and wandering to the bathroom or meetings, you're so stationary. You need to move more, and maybe think about your needs for a change, instead of just your clients'.

"People like you work too hard, not that I don't appreciate your amazing work ethic and accomplishments so far. But if you're not careful, you could work so hard that you forget to take care of yourself, and before you know it, you're dead."

He laughed. "That's a little drastic, don't you think?"

"Not really. I'm not saying you should slack off entirely.

I'm saying taking a break to stretch your legs isn't a bad thing."

"Why do you care so much about my health? Aren't you the one who keeps telling me how temporary our arrangement is?" He looked down at his food immediately after speaking.

"I'm surprised you don't get it, after everything with your dad."

Sawyer clenched his jaw. "What does my father have to do with anything?"

"I don't want to see you end up like he did…"

He put down his food and leveled his gaze at her. "My father died because of a boating accident."

"Because he had a massive heart attack while on the lake and crashed the boat," she said softly. "I don't want to see you work yourself to death."

"My father's death isn't your concern," he said, barely getting the words through his tight jaw. "He did everything right and still died, so what good is worrying about the future when I might not even have one?"

The thought that Sawyer didn't believe he had a future because he was destined for the same fate as his father made her chest burn. She ate quietly for a minute, afraid to say the wrong thing and piss him off more. It wasn't her intention. "Listen, I wasn't trying to put my nose where it didn't belong, and I shouldn't have brought up your dad. It is none of my business how you live your life. From now on, I'll stay out of it."

He sighed. "No, you're right. I work too much, and lately I've been playing too little, but that's only because you've been around."

So I'm the problem? Nice.

"Sorry. In less than two months you can have your precious playtime back, without me in your way. I won't remind you that this whole thing was your idea."

"I didn't mean that the way it sounded. I like having you around." He dropped his empty containers back into the bag. "I work hard because I have to. That's all. If I don't…"

He trailed off, looking out the doorway into the rest of the office, and all the empty, darkened cubicles. Sadness she hadn't seen before glimmered in his eyes. "If I don't, I could lose everything."

He grabbed her hand and pulled her up from the table. The physical contact warmed her skin. "Let's get to work so we can get the hell out of here."

"Sounds good." She joined him at his desk, leaning over his shoulder to read his computer screen. The scent of his cologne infiltrated her senses, making her head spin and a pressure build low in her abdomen. She sucked in a quick breath then stepped away.

"Can we turn the monitor so I can sit in a chair?" She grabbed one and pulled it around to his side of the desk, close to him, but hopefully with enough distance between them that she wouldn't have to smell his delicious scent anymore.

"Better?" he asked, twisting the monitor.

"Much. It hurt my back to bend over you like that. Not that I was bent over. Just leaning, really."

Crap. Why hadn't she come up with a better excuse than her back hurting? Her back was fine. It was her libido getting in the way. If her stupid, horny, girl hormones would get under control, she'd be fine.

He raised an eyebrow at her. "All this talk about you bending over me makes me want to bend you over my desk. Not that I would, what with your back hurting and all. I will point out, conversations like this one do nothing to help me stick to our strict 'no touching' policy. And frankly, it's mean for you to tease me this way."

"I…I wasn't teasing," she squeaked out between tight breaths. She may have daydreamed about Sawyer, his desk, and a little less clothing a time or two, but she never would have said it out loud for him to hear. "I was letting you know why I moved to the chair. It's not my fault you have a perpetually dirty mind."

"If you'd get over your hang up about us, I guarantee you'd rather enjoy my dirty mind, and all the places it takes me. Just because you've decided we're off-limits doesn't mean my mind has to agree."

He turned back to the computer monitor as if their conversation had been nothing more than regular office chatter. Meanwhile, her panties were distinctly more uncomfortable and she fought the urge to squirm in her chair. God only knew what response that action might elicit from him.

He took a few minutes to show her everything he had so far. He'd done a great job already. The marketing was clean and the message was clear. Use the products, get healthy, stay healthy. And with many of the products being designed for children, she couldn't imagine a parent who wouldn't want that for their child.

"So, what do we need to do next, since this already looks awesome?"

"I wish I knew. Technically, this is all Marcus asked for, and while I think it's great, I'm worried it's not enough. I feel like we need something that will set us apart from the competition—an idea or twist no one else has thought of yet. Something that will make buyers in the States, which has potential to be his biggest market, take notice of his product despite all the others out there."

Olivia studied the mock-ups for the shakes, bars, and snacks that Marcus wanted to sell to the world. Full of vitamins, minerals, enzymes, and electrolytes, they basically had everything a person could want in a health food.

She took a deep swig from her aluminum water bottle and leaned back in the chair, contemplating what she would look for in a product like that. How would she make her decision to buy it, instead of the competition? Tapping her foot while thinking, her eye was drawn to her new vegan shoes, the ones she'd spontaneously purchased because she couldn't resist how cute they were, how comfortable they were, and how awesome it was to have cruelty-free shoes.

"That's it!" she exclaimed, sitting forward.

"What's it?"

"I know you already think I'm an environmentalist hippie or something, but save your snap judgments and hear me out."

"Of course."

"Of course, as in I'm a hippie environmentalist, or of course, as in you'll listen?"

He squished his lips together, shrugged innocently, then motioned for her to go on.

She narrowed her eyes for a second, knowing he was being elusive. "The packaging. We should suggest changing it before it goes into production. These plastic bottled drinks are all individually wrapped in more plastic, then boxed in cardboard. Skipping the plastic wrapping would cut back on a lot of waste. Then if we could even find a way to make those ring holders that are always on six-packs of soda out of a different, biodegradable material, then we could get rid of the box too."

Ideas tumbled out of her so fast, her mouth could barely keep up. Less packaging, different materials, starting with post-consumer recycled products to begin with—it would all lead to a better carbon footprint and would go a long way to proving Marcus wasn't in it to make money and actually cared about the health of his customers, and of the planet.

"A healthier you, right from the ground up," she said, finally pausing long enough to take a sip of water.

"Wow." Sawyer leaned back in his chair, staring at her.

Her excitement fizzled. "Good wow or bad wow?"

A grin spread across his face. "Great wow." He shook his head, his eyes never leaving hers. "You're absolutely amazing."

He turned back to his computer and typed everything she'd said into their file, noting all the changes that would need to be made, stats they'd have to research, and anything else they'd need to pull together before their meeting with Marcus the following week.

"Let's get out of here," he said, after shutting off the monitor. "We've definitely done enough for today, thanks to you. Tomorrow I'll fill in the rest of the team and we'll get to work with a fresh new focus."

As his chair swiveled around so he could face her, their knees brushed together. Tingles danced a path up her legs, all the way to the junction between her thighs. Thoughts of him between her legs, in his office, made her head swim.

He squeezed her knee, and she couldn't stop herself from imagining his hand sliding across her skin to find her throbbing center.

She licked her lips, fighting the urge to spread her legs and invite him in for another go. It wouldn't accomplish anything but temporary relief and long-term heartache. Even as her head knew the facts, her body only knew the feeling, and it definitely craved his touch again.

He peered deep into her eyes then stood, pulling her up with him. His hands on her shoulders, he spoke with such genuine admiration and appreciation in his voice that an overwhelming sense of pride consumed her. "You really are such an asset to this team. Being more eco-conscious is exactly the kind of thing Marcus is going to respond to. I don't know how you came up with the idea, but you're brilliant."

"It was two things," she said, nervous at his closeness but not doing anything to change it. "One, he mentioned something at the gala that led me to believe he'd care about his company's carbon footprint."

"The other inspiration?"

"My shoes." She glanced down quickly at the black flats. "They're vegan."

"Your shoes don't eat meat?" he asked, chuckling.

"No, they're made from cruelty-free products. It made me think, if a shoe company can make vegan shoes, surely we can improve on the proposed over-packaging of Marcus' product."

"Every time I think I have you figured out, you do something else to amaze me." Taking her hand, he led her out of the office. They settled into the car and she was thankful he needed his hands free to drive. Any more contact and she might not be able to stop from doing something she'd regret, like kissing him again. Or worse.

"Everyone's getting together at the cabin for the long weekend," he said.

"I'm sure they'll have a great time."

"We're going too, of course."

She forced her gaze away from the twinkling city at night to face him instead. Was he suggesting they try to fool his family for an entire long weekend? "Do we have to? Not that I don't like your family or anything, but three or four days away together is a long time to act like we're in love."

"True, but we always help Gran and Gramps get the cabin ready for the summer season."

A few more family-time obligations acting like a couple and they may as well be one. The thought sent a pang of longing through her, but she shook it off before it could take hold. Flirting and faking it with Sawyer was one thing, but falling for him was completely unacceptable. But did she really have any choice to not go? She'd agreed to this arrangement knowing what it would mean, and now she had to play along. It wasn't right to refuse him when going was critical to his getting the cabin.

She sighed, hating her inner logic. If she really were his girlfriend, she'd want to go. It wasn't as if he asked something out of the ordinary or unreasonable.

"Fine, I'll go."

"Well, don't sound so thrilled about it."

"I'm not, but this is what I signed up for, so I'll do it."

"It's not like I'm asking you to walk into a lake filled with piranhas. It's a weekend with my family at a beautiful cabin."

He smiled as if seeing the cabin in his mind. If she wasn't mistaken, his eyes looked moist and almost teary.

She sighed and bit the inside of her cheek to keep from saying something stupid. Of course he would have mixed emotions about the cabin — it was home to him, but the lake was also the site of his parent's accident. He was lucky to have somewhere that felt like home, not that she'd say that to him. The last place she'd called home had been sold after the divorce. She'd give anything to have that kind of structure and stability in her life again.

She might not be able to have that for herself, but she could damn well suck it up and make sure Sawyer got the cabin he so obviously loved. And being a part of his family, even temporarily, wasn't so bad either.

Chapter Thirteen

Sawyer's foot stung when it connected with the ball. Not only was he tired as all hell tonight, but his technique sucked too.

Aidan barely ducked out of the way before it zinged past his head. "Watch it. We're on the same team, and it's practice. Take it easy."

"Sorry, man." Sawyer shook his head and tried to walk off the pain throbbing in his foot. If he didn't start paying more attention to his form, he would end up hurt and out of the next game. That couldn't happen, not when they were up against W-Cubed. Those web design geeks kicked ass.

Sawyer wandered over to the bench where the girls sat on the sidelines, once again noting Olivia's absence, and grabbed his water bottle. When she'd said she wanted to sit this practice out, he'd happily agreed. He'd needed a break from her, the constant reminder of what he couldn't have, but he'd never thought he'd miss seeing her. It was almost as if part of him was absent.

The last few weeks had been long, grueling almost. Work had been tedious and frustrating until the night before when Olivia had come up with her great new ideas for the Marcus project. As he ran the length of the soccer field with the boys, he hoped it would help him sleep tonight. He hadn't slept well or felt like himself since Olivia said no.

He'd gotten a taste of her sweet tongue dancing in his mouth, the caress of her hands on his body, the heat deep between her legs surrounding him in pure ecstasy. God damn it, he wanted more.

Torture was not part of their agreement, but that's exactly what she was doing to him. His balls felt like a pair of grapes drying in the scorching desert sun. He needed a release...but not just any release. He only wanted Olivia. More than that, she saw who he really was and what he was missing in life, and, against his better judgment, he was starting to see it, too—he needed her. Not only in his bed, but in his life in general.

When she'd said no to more intimacy, she'd put up a wall between them, cutting him off from more than her body. It was a cold shower to his mind, too. Her distance made him anxious, uncomfortable, and irritable. And it annoyed him that he cared so much.

He took a long gulp of his water. The ball slammed against him, sending him to the ground. "Damn it. That hurt." He clutched his side and coughed as he got to his feet.

"What the hell, Sawyer?" Brian smacked him on the shoulder. "Get your head out of your ass already. I'm not here to waste time."

"Sorry. I didn't see the ball coming." He straightened his

spine and stood tall, showing he wasn't fazed by the hit, even if his kidney felt like it might be bleeding.

"You've been distracted all night." Jason motioned toward the girls. "What, you can't play unless your girl is here to show off for?"

"Why isn't Olivia here?" Stacy asked. "I was looking forward to chatting with her again."

"She had other things to do."

"Trouble in paradise already?" Brian teased.

"We're fine. Life is blissfully wonderful."

The guys cheered and whistled, annoying him further. He should've kept his mouth shut.

"Now we know you're lying," Kennedy said. She winked, deviously. "If she's cut you off, you know I'm always here for you."

"That must be it. You always get messy on the field when you haven't had any recently." Chad nodded confidently. "It's gotta be—what, a week, maybe two—given your level of distraction and lack of skill."

"I'm not cut off. Things are great in the bedroom."

Aidan shot him a murderous look that said it better all be part of the scam.

"Just in the bedroom? Now I know there's something wrong." Chad and Jason laughed.

"Enough. She's still my little sister and I won't listen to you jackasses talk about her like that," Aidan said.

The guys took the hint and ran to the other end of the field to get back into practice with the rest of the team, while Aidan and Sawyer made their way slowly over to join them. Sawyer didn't want to look at him. His friend was too perceptive to lie to.

"I'm sure I don't need to ask this, but the guys aren't right, are they? Your poor performance doesn't have anything to do with my sister, does it?"

"They're right."

"Then you better start running because I *will* use you as a punching bag."

"They're right that I've been cut off. I mean it's not like I can go to the bar with you when she's supposed to be my girlfriend. So excuse me if I'm a little...pent up."

There, that sounded convincing. Perfectly logical, too.

"So you're not sleeping with my sister?" Aidan folded his arms across his chest, his stance wide.

"I'm not doing anything with her."

Not anymore. Thanks to her new, more rigid "no touching" policy. Knowing it was for the best didn't quell his desire to be with her.

Aidan held his gaze and Sawyer prayed his voice had been convincing. If he had to answer any more questions about his relationship, he was bound to slip up.

"I won't hesitate to protect my sister, especially from you. I won't see her get hurt by some cocky playboy again."

Annoyance put him on edge. What, he wasn't good enough for Aidan's precious little sister? "Last I checked, she was all grown up and could protect herself."

"Don't test my patience, Sawyer."

"Ditto, Aidan."

"I just got my sister back, dude. I can't have her running off around the world again because you're horny."

"I don't want her leaving again, either."

"Then back off and keep up your end of the deal." Aidan sprinted toward the team, leaving Sawyer practically growling.

He jogged after him while whispering to himself. "Don't forget, big bro, the deal was between me and Olivia. If we want to screw around, *again*, there's not a damn thing you can do about it."

...

Olivia sipped her wine cooler and watched her brother work in the kitchen. She should get up from her stool at the counter and help, but really, how hard was spaghetti and garlic bread?

"Ready to move back in yet?" Aidan asked, stirring the pot of noodles boiling on the stove. "You're always welcome on my couch if you're ready to move on with your life for real and end this stupid game you're playing with Sawyer."

"And give up my comfy bed at his place? No way. Besides, this is my real life right now."

"You really think this thing with Sawyer is the right way to get ahead?" Aidan tasted the sauce then added another pinch of oregano.

"Sterling Enterprises is a great company, and it will look awesome on my resume. Why wouldn't I work for him?"

"Because you're working for him and living with him. And by the looks of things, getting pretty cozy with him, too." He raised his eyebrows, challenging her to contradict the statement.

She wouldn't fall for his trap. Sawyer would never have told Aidan about what happened after the gala, so anything her brother thought he knew was only speculation. "What are you talking about? I'm not getting cozy with him. We're friends, business associates, and roommates. That's it."

Aidan leaned on the counter, pinning her with his gaze. "Who are you trying to convince, me or yourself?"

She took another few sips of her drink, tying to buy herself a couple of seconds to think.

True, she had gotten pretty damn cozy with Sawyer the night of the gala, and while it had been awesome, it was also a mistake. She knew that.

True, she'd thought about going to bed with him again, but she was *not* going to.

True, she would never admit anything to Aidan, not only because he would kill Sawyer, but because verifying her "coziness" with him would also be admitting she'd had sex. That was not a conversation she was prepared to have with her brother, now or ever. Some things were much better left a mystery.

"There's nothing going on between Sawyer and me. I swear." She hopped off the stool and went to the stove. Maybe if she moved around, he'd forget what they were talking about and move on to another topic. Tasting the sauce, she groaned. Aidan wasn't the world's best chef, but he could make a mean sauce. "This is delicious. Can we eat now?"

Aidan fixed them each a plate of food and refilled their drinks. She missed their family-style dinners together. Sure, it wasn't a big gathering like at Sawyer's grandparents' place, but it was still nice, and it was hers.

"Thanks for having me over. This is kind of nice. You and me, hanging out."

"Any time, little sis. But next time you have to cook because this is basically the only meal I know how to make."

"Don't you ever cook dinner for girls?" she asked, then

sucked a noodle through her lips.

"Yeah, sometimes." He shrugged.

"Well, don't you ever cook for the same girl more than once? You don't always feed her spaghetti, do you? Don't you need at least a few recipes in your cookbook?"

"One, I'm a guy. I don't have a cookbook." He smirked while she rolled her eyes. Typical. "And two, I'm a bachelor by choice. I don't tend to need more than one recipe. They aren't around long enough for me to cook for them twice."

She smacked her brother on the arm. "Pig. Just love 'em and dump 'em, huh?"

"No. Dumping them would imply we were in a relationship to begin with, which we never are. I'm like Sawyer. I don't do relationships."

The reminder of Sawyer's beliefs about marriage stung, but she pushed the feeling aside as much as she could. "And why not? Our parents didn't die young and leave behind orphans."

"No, ours got divorced out of the blue. Why would I ever sign up for that?"

She scoffed. "Lots of marriages last forever. That's why they sell fortieth wedding anniversary cards at the drug store."

"Who buys paper cards anymore? Send an e-card like a normal person. I mean, I know you were in all these weird countries for a long time, but get with the decade."

"I'm perfectly normal."

"Sure you are." He laughed and dodged out of the way as she tried to smack him again. "I'm not against all marriage as a whole. I just know it's not for me. When the likelihood of divorce is so high, why bother with all that legality when simply dating lets you split without the mess."

"Not all marriages end in divorce."

"But all divorces begin with a marriage."

"You're irritating."

"And I'm right. Trust me, Sawyer feels the same. Getting involved with him is a sure fire way to end up hurt and alone." He put his hand on hers and squeezed. "I don't want to see that happen to you again."

Olivia bit back a sudden prickle of tears. She knew Aidan was right about everything, but that didn't take the sting out of the truth. Why did she keep getting involved with guys who couldn't commit?

She forced every ounce of confidence she could muster into her voice. "Thanks for worrying about me, but you don't need to. I'm good. For the first time in a long time, I'm on my way to where I want to be and nothing, not Sawyer or anyone else like him, is going to get in my way."

If only she believed her words with as much conviction as she'd said them.

Chapter Fourteen

Sawyer swallowed the ball of anxiety rising in his throat. He always felt the same way coming to the cabin. His grandparents had done their best to give him a family life, and the cabin did feel like home more than anywhere else, but he couldn't shake the undertone of sadness he still felt, even after all these years.

And yet, he still couldn't imagine letting the cabin go to someone else. Aside from Gran and Gramps, no one would care about this place more than he did. No one would do a better job of honoring his parents' memory.

"Ready?" he asked, as the car made its way around the last bend.

Olivia smiled. "I'm looking forward to seeing Gran again. I wish I had a grandmother like her."

Sawyer remembered that she and Aidan had lost their grandparents early in life. He'd never even considered how she would feel about becoming close to his grandparents.

Has she been enjoying it, or suffering? His heart sank. He'd have to make sure she enjoyed herself this weekend. It was her vacation, too.

"Besides, I'm ready for a break from the city. Bring on the open spaces, fresh air, and relaxation."

"Prepping the cabin for summer is usually a fair amount of work, not that you have to do any of it. I can get the deck chairs cleaned up first thing so you can hang out and relax."

"Or you could give me a list so I can help out, too. I can't sit around all weekend while everyone else works."

Of course she would insist on helping. She wasn't the kind of girl to take it easy while others did all the hard work. Olivia was a girl who got stuff done, not someone who sat around all the time.

He pulled up in front of the cabin. "We're here."

Taking her hand in one of his, he grabbed their bags in the other, and they made their way inside. What was calm and peaceful outside was mildly chaotic inside. Even though the place had been updated for year-round use, there were still dozens of tasks that had to be completed, inside and out, every spring and fall. Even with the renovations, the cabin was old and the seasons were hard on the structure. Every year there were new things to fix, clean, and replace.

"Good, you're finally here. We were starting to worry." Gran kissed Sawyer on the cheek, while Olivia got a bear hug. A tiny squeak escaped her as Gran released her. "Oh, dear. Guess I don't know my own strength."

"You're tougher than you look, that's for sure," she said.

"Damn right I am." Gran looked around conspiratorially and dropped her voice to a whisper. "But don't tell Gramps that. If he knew, he might make me start bringing in the grocery bags and taking out the trash." With a laugh, she wandered into the kitchen, waving them toward the back of the cabin. "You'll be in Sawyer's old room."

He groaned. Not good. It was the smallest bedroom, tucked into the very back corner of the cabin. It only had room for a full-sized bed, not a queen like the other rooms. The only redeeming quality was the second entrance to the deck. If the room got too stuffy, they could open the sliding door and get the breeze off the lake.

He led her to the room, already guessing her reaction. He closed the door behind him so they could have a moment in private.

"One bed. Again?"

"Every room only has one bed. At least it's only for three nights. We've shared a bed before."

"Yes, and we remember how well that worked out last time, don't we?"

He held her gaze as his thoughts flittered back to the gala, taking Olivia to bed, holding her in his arms, kissing her, touching her, tasting her.

"Worked out pretty damn well in my opinion." He smirked as she rolled her eyes. "I'll stay on my side if you stay on yours."

She sighed. "You better."

• • •

Olivia sprayed the hose at the soapy layer of filth she'd scrubbed off the patio furniture. Sawyer and Gran had tried to tell her that she was a guest, and therefore should just grab a towel to cover one of the chairs until they got them cleaned, and relax for a while. She'd asked for a bucket and soap instead, insisting that if she was Sawyer's girlfriend, then that made her almost family and they needed to stop treating her like she was breakable.

Tyler's wife was the fragile pregnant one, not her. Olivia had more than enough energy to be useful, and eventually she'd convinced them she was only doing Sophia's share of the work.

Now, a couple of hours later, she was rinsing off the last chair on the deck so that it would have time to dry in the sun before anyone wanted to use them tonight to watch the sunset. Not bad for an afternoon's work.

She loved it here. The quiet, the fresh air, the family buzzing around, working on the house—all of it felt wonderful to be a part of. The idea that this might be her only long weekend at the cabin made her heart hurt.

"Where are you off to?" she asked Tyler as he came out of the cabin with a handful of cash and a purposeful stride.

"Gramps needs to borrow a power washer from the neighbor Ralph to clean the siding, so I'm running over to pick it up."

"Want some company?" she asked. "I'm done here and I don't have anything else on my to-do list yet."

"Sure."

She followed him off the deck and turned for the cars, only to have him head toward the lake. "Where are you going?"

"To the neighbor's. They're on the other side of the lake. This is the fastest way." He hopped onto the boat moored to the pier and extended his hand to her, helping her step onto the moving surface.

As he untied the ropes, she settled herself into one of the seats and looked around. "Where are the life jackets?"

"We don't need them. We won't be out long. You're not afraid of the water, are you?" He gunned the engine and the boat lurched forward.

A shriek escaped her as she clung to the sides of her chair. He let off the throttle for a moment and she fought to regain her composure. He looked at her and chuckled, then sent the boat shooting forward again. By the time they made it to the "neighbor's" cottage, she felt as if she'd run a marathon in an August heat wave. When Tyler left to collect the power washer, she slumped in her chair and thought about what alternative mode of transportation she could take to get back to the cabin. Surely, there was a taxi service out here, or maybe she could just walk. It couldn't be that far, right?

Olivia tried to remain calm. "He never told me boating was part of the deal. This was supposed to be a relaxing trip, that's all. He never said anything about life-risking boating rides being part of the plan."

"What was that?" Tyler asked, as he heaved the machine into the boat and secured it with a couple of bungee cords. "What plan? Were you guys supposed to do something in town today?"

"No. We didn't have plans. I don't know what you're talking about," she said, still feeling completely off-kilter and absolutely unable to deal with Tyler or his questions. "Can you tell me how to get to the nearest road and I'll flag down a taxi?"

He laughed. Hard. "You can't be serious? No taxis here."

"I'll walk."

"Don't be silly. You just need to get a feel for the water, that's all. I'll take you on the scenic route and by the time we get back, you'll be one with the lake."

"I'm not sure I want to be one with the lake!" she yelled as the boat lurched forward.

If he heard her words, he gave no indication. This time, instead of heading directly back across the middle of the lake like they had before, he skirted around the perimeter, zigzagging.

"Slow down!" she yelled.

He grinned over his shoulder. "We aren't even going fast yet."

As they rounded a bend in the lake, another boat crossed their path, not nearly far enough ahead to be comforting. She screamed as they hit the wake of the other watercraft and she bounced in her seat. When the bouncing finally subsided, he turned the wheel hard, spinning the boat to the left and sending a huge splash of water shooting into the sky.

A minute later he cut the engine and was tying the boat to the pier.

Olivia had barely registered the boat had stopped moving when she heard yelling. Sawyer was on the pier, his fists balled into the front of Tyler's shirt, pulling him off balance.

"What the fuck do you think you're doing running off with Olivia like that?"

"I didn't run off with her. She asked to come with me." Tyler pulled out of Sawyer's grip.

"You should've told me you were taking her out on the boat!" Sawyer fisted his hands at his sides.

"And if I had you wouldn't have let her come."

He laughed, but it didn't sound like it came from humor.

It sounded like a man who was on the edge of losing control. "Damn right. And it seems perfectly reasonable, given how you came streaking into the dock with her screaming her head off!"

"How was I supposed to know you'd find a woman as afraid of the lake as you are? If she didn't want to go for a ride, she shouldn't have asked me to take her."

"You should know better than to act like a punk on the water."

"Sawyer, it's okay," she said, finally finding her voice.

In an instant, she was pulled onto the pier and into Sawyer's arms. He kissed her, hard, on the mouth, and everything else around her disappeared. When he pulled back, he rested his forehead against hers, staring into her eyes with concern. It was as if she could see into the depths of his soul to his deepest, darkest pain.

"Are you hurt?" he whispered.

She shook her head and bit her lip, urging the tears she felt building to subside so he'd believe her. She wasn't hurt, just shaken up by the whole experience and more than a little embarrassed at the scene she'd unintentionally caused.

"If anything had happened to you out there…" His voice broke and he cleared his throat, then he turned to face Tyler. "Never again. Do you hear me?"

Before he answered, Sawyer was leading her back to the house, his strong hand gripped around hers.

• • •

By the time he got Olivia alone again, she'd helped Gran fix a delicious dinner for everyone and was relaxing with a cup of hot tea on the deck, watching the sunset over the lake as if she hadn't almost died on the water earlier.

"Dinner was delicious," he said, joining her. Tension radiated through his shoulders as he rolled them, urging the muscles to relax. He'd spent the day fixing shingles that had come loose over the winter, cleaning up the yard, scrubbing a year's worth of grime from the siding.

Oh, and reliving his parents' accident. Nothing major.

"How are you doing?" he asked.

"Better than you, by the looks of it. What's wrong with your back?"

"I'm used to sitting at a desk, not hammering shingles." He shrugged then winced. Olivia watched as he attempted to rub the tension out of his shoulders. He finally gave up and sighed with defeat, unable to relieve his discomfort.

"Come here." She motioned him over to sit between her legs, facing the lake. "Let me massage your shoulders."

For a nanosecond he toyed with the idea of refusing, then peeled himself out of the chair to sit on the deck instead. He couldn't remember the last time he'd had a shoulder rub and he wasn't about to miss out on the opportunity now.

As her fingers pressed into his tight muscles, he groaned. Her hands on his body felt good, and not because of what they did for his tension. She hadn't been close to him like this for so long. He missed having her near.

He wasn't tired, but he suddenly couldn't wait to climb into bed for the night.

Her fingers moved in slow circles, stretching out the tightness. With each press and release, he sank against her more, trying hard not to think about how he was currently between her legs. The last time he'd been between them had been incredible. He could imagine it would be even better the next time—not that she planned on giving him a next time. He'd have to see what he could do about that.

She stroked up the back of his neck and into his hair, then slowly made her way back down to his shoulders. Over and over again, she teased him with her touch. He longed to have her touch him other places with this same kind of attention and time commitment.

"God, that feels good, sugar," he said with a sigh of deep pleasure. "Don't stop."

Her hands stilled, resting on his shoulders. "Sorry. My hands are sore."

He mumbled his thanks and twisted slightly so he could rest his head on her thigh. Peering out over the water, he could think of nowhere else he'd rather be than with her in this moment.

He'd never really been a guy who enjoyed sitting around taking in the scenery at the cabin. He'd rather be out doing something—swimming, drinking, boating on the lake, or making a bonfire. But in his current position, he didn't want to be anywhere else, with anyone else. He felt perfectly content exactly where he was—with Olivia.

When Gran suggested dessert a few short minutes later, he could've killed her. Olivia was the first to jump at the chance to get everyone a slice of pie and refill of their coffees. She seemed to love helping Gran in the kitchen. He'd heard them in there earlier, chatting and laughing, and it had stirred something up inside him, but he hadn't figured out what it was yet, exactly.

After a large slice of apple pie and ice cream, she insisted on washing the dishes, and he took the opportunity to bring in more firewood from the stack out back. The weather was warm during the day, but the nights still dipped into the forties. Gran liked to warm the place up with a fire the last hour or two before everyone turned in for the night. He'd volunteered for duty that evening.

As he lit the fire, Olivia excused herself for bed. He didn't try to stop her since he could see the dark shadows under her eyes already.

"No cuddling on the couch with the little lady tonight?" Tyler asked, flopping down in the armchair a little while later. "Isn't that what people in love are supposed to do? Cuddle in front of the fireplace."

Sawyer fisted his hands and relaxed them again before speaking. The last thing he needed was to deal with Tyler. He didn't have the energy after the long day. "She's still recovering from her boat ride with you."

"That spin around the lake really got you worked up, didn't it? Or was that tough guy overreaction for Gran's benefit? Still trying to convince us all that you actually love her, huh?"

"My feelings for her are none of your business," he said in a low voice, barely controlled. "Instead of worrying about my relationship, why don't you go take care of your pregnant wife?"

On cue, Sophia called from the bedroom. "Babe, can you bring me a water?" Tyler looked as if he wanted to say more, but instead rose and fetched his wife a drink, leaving Sawyer alone with only the crackle of the fire for company.

Did he love Olivia? No, but he sure as hell had been scared when he'd heard her screams coming from the lake. Was that simply a symptom of dealing with his parents' accident after all these years?

He wandered out to the deck and leaned on the railing, staring out at the black water and the starlight twinkling on the surface. The cabin was the place he felt closest to his parents—as if they were still out there on the water somewhere and if he waited long enough they might come home.

"What are you doing out here?" Olivia said, joining him.

"The fire's already smoldering. A little longer and it'll be safe to leave it for the night." He breathed in the cool night air, feeling like he could never get enough of it after all the time he spent in the city.

Shivering beside him, Olivia rubbed her hands up and down her bare arms. She'd come out in her pajamas, which weren't warm enough for the temperature drop at night. "It's beautiful out here. Peaceful."

He slipped an arm around her shoulders, pulling her into his embrace. She stiffened. "Just trying to keep you from freezing, sugar. I can't have you freezing out here or Gran will never let me hear the end of it." She relaxed and he went back to watching the water.

This, he could get used to.

"I can see why you like it out here."

"It's one of my favorite places. I'm glad you're here to see it."

"Me, too."

"I'm sorry about my cousin. He was completely out of line. If I'd known, I would never have let you go."

"You can't stop me from doing something I want to do, and I wanted to go along for the ride. If it were up to you, I would've sat around on my ass all day reading."

"But it's such a nice ass," he teased, fighting the urge

to touch the anatomy in question. He sighed. "I don't mean to be overbearing or a tyrant of a boyfriend. It's just this lake and the accident and you… I guess I lost my mind for a second."

"I get it, and if I'd known Tyler was taking me for a joyride, I never would've gone."

He ran his hand up her shoulder and into her hair, toying with the silky strands. "If only I could forget. It's this place. It does something to me. Makes me face the things I don't necessarily want to deal with. But yet, I love it here."

"I completely understand why you would do anything you can to keep it. But even if Tyler gets it, won't you still be able to come here once in a while?"

He shrugged. "I doubt it. Tyler is very possessive of his things. I can't say for sure, but from the way he's acted so far, I'd say the cabin is just another possession to him, and one he won't be inclined to share."

She peered up at him, twisting slightly in his arms. Her gaze darted into the house, then her hand cupped his jaw, coaxing him toward her. When her lips pressed to his in a light kiss, it felt as if everything in his world clicked into place—her, him, the cool breeze blowing off the lake, the stars in all their glory, and the sweetest, most delicious mouth on his.

Before the kiss could go further, she pulled away. "Gran's watching. I think it's time for bed." She slipped her hand into his and pulled him to the door leading directly to their bedroom.

Safely in their room, Olivia crawled under the covers and picked up her book as if she hadn't just kissed him.

He slipped off his shirt and dropped it to the floor.

"Thanks."

"For what?" she asked, setting her book face down on the blankets.

"For that, out there. You didn't have to do that to convince Gran."

"I know. I wanted…" She bit her lip and picked up her book again, focusing on it. "Never mind."

Wanted what? To kiss me?

As much as this whole relationship was an act with her, he enjoyed having her here. She fit in like she'd always been a part of the family. It was…nice. Too nice, probably. The kind of nice that would cause him problems later on.

But I wanted that kiss, too. And another one.

His shorts joined his shirt on the floor. No point in trying to prevent them from wrinkling since they were beyond filthy after all the work he'd done today. He climbed into bed with just his boxers on.

"You're not coming to bed like that, are you?" she asked, eyeing him from over the top of her book. Her gaze traveled the length of his body and his dick twitched to life. He quickly pulled the blanket over himself, ignoring his awakening desire.

"I am," he said. "I usually sleep naked. I could do that if you prefer."

Her breasts strained against the thin tank top material, her nipples already beaded.

Fuck me! He wanted to be with her again so badly it almost hurt. He definitely wouldn't mind sleeping naked if there was a possibility it would lead to more interesting nighttime activities with Olivia. All she had to do was say the word.

Her breath hitched. Instead of answering him, she put her book on the nightstand, shut off her light, and laid down on her side. But she faced toward him, not away like he'd expected.

He sank deeper in the blankets and turned toward her. Her eyes were closed but not yet peaceful. Her breaths still came quickly, wavering softly. A strand of hair across her cheek caught his attention. Without thinking, he tucked it behind her ear.

Her features relaxed and the creases beside her eyes softened with his touch as he trailed his fingertips along her jaw. Her lips parted with a tiny gasp. He stroked the line of her bottom lip and waited her to say something, or open her eyes to meet his gaze, but she remained still, ignoring his advances.

Finally, he withdrew his hand and rested it on the bed between them, disappointed at her lack of interest in his touch. A moment later her hand crept out from beneath the covers and settled next to his. For a second her finger gently swept across his knuckles.

As he listened to her breathing even out in the darkness cocooning them from the rest of the world, he wondered how he'd gotten to this point. He'd never been comfortable sleeping with a woman when it meant actually sleeping. He was a "*sleep* with a woman and then bail to head home to his own bed" kind of guy. Yet tonight, he couldn't think of anywhere else he wanted to be. Except maybe wrapped around her body...

Damn it! He wasn't supposed to want her this much. He *shouldn't* want her this much. It was too complicated for both of them.

Chapter Fifteen

Olivia downed half a bottle of water with the last bite of her sandwich. Everyone had taken a break to eat before getting started with the afternoon work. As she cleaned her dishes in the sink, Sawyer walked in with his. She took them and added them to the bubbles.

"Thank you for helping Gran today. She never complains, but I know she's finding the work harder this year. I know she appreciated your help."

She'd worked non-stop all morning—not that she was complaining—with Gran in the small garden on the side of the house. Just before noon, they'd gotten the last of the seeds planted and the weeds cleaned out. It would still take some weekly maintenance by Gran, but she should get a nice harvest after all their hard work today.

"No problem. I'm happy to help and keep busy. And I liked working with Gran in the garden. It was more fun than work, actually. She's such a nice lady." Feeling like a part of the Sterling family was a perk of their arrangement she'd never expected, and she was reveling in it for as long as she could, even if it meant getting dirt under her nails. "What else can I do this afternoon?"

"I'd love it if you'd do me a favor," he said.

"Name it." She put the last of the plates onto the dish rack to dry and let the sink drain while she wiped her hands.

"Go sit in the sun and read for a while," he said. "I know you want to help, but you've already done more than your share. I want you to have some time to relax this weekend."

"Will you join me? You need time to relax too you know." If it was good for her, it was good for him. Only the man's work ethic—at his regular job and here, apparently— continually got in the way.

"I need to finish putting on the new window screens," he said. When she arched an eyebrow, challenging him silently, he sighed and she knew she'd won. "I'll try to finish up and join you later. Okay?"

"Deal." She grabbed an apple from the fridge, craving the crisp, sweet freshness, and gave it a quick rinse as he walked out the door. "But if Gran asks me for help again later, I'm going to stop that whole relaxing thing you mentioned."

He chuckled as he walked outside, leaving her alone in the kitchen. If she had some free time on her hands, maybe she'd run down to the lake and wash the garden off herself with a swim.

Digging a swimsuit out of her bag, she quickly changed then grabbed a towel, sunscreen, her water bottle, and a novel before going out to the deck. The cabin overlooked the lake, which sparkled invitingly as the sunlight reflected off the surface. Wanting a little privacy, she found a tiny, mostly overgrown path and dodged plants along the way. Moments later it opened up to another lake access area, only this one seemed secluded and unused. The grass was long, the small sandy beach was littered with driftwood, and a boat lay upside down just above the shoreline. By how far it was sunken into the sand, she guessed it hadn't been used in years.

Figuring she was safe to relax there, she cleared away a section of debris from the beach and unfolded her towel. She sat for a while, peering out over the lake, enjoying the gentle lapping of the waves on the beach. All the tension and stress weighing her down for the last couple of months melted away, and a sense of calmness settled in.

Soon her skin radiated with heat from soaking in the sun, and the water called to her. She stood and pulled the light sundress she'd worn over her head, laying it carefully on the towel, tucking it under her book so it wouldn't blow away in the breeze.

Shrieking as frigid water splashed over her ankles, she considered turning around and heading for her towel again, but without an option for shade, this was the only way to cool off.

"Holy mother of God, it's freezing." She cupped water in her hands and attempted to acclimate herself to the temperature by pouring it over her arms and legs. It didn't work. Instead she simultaneously shivered and burned up.

"You're doing it wrong."

She screamed and twisted, almost losing her balance. "What are you doing here?"

"I could ask you the same thing," Sawyer said.

"You told me to relax, so I came for a swim. I thought you'd be happy I was finally out of the way."

"Not that you're overly dramatic or anything."

She shook her head and put her hands on her hips. "I wasn't trying to be dramatic. And I didn't intend to pull you away from whatever it was you were doing."

He moved to her towel and toed off his shoes. "I know you didn't, but I noticed you disappear down my trail and I figured I should come check on you."

Why did he take off his shoes? He's not staying.

"Well, I'm okay, if you want to go back."

Hint, hint.

"The lake looks pretty irresistible." His gaze was solidly locked on hers and nowhere near the lake. "I think I might stay and take a dip, enjoy the sunshine and nice scenery for a bit before I get back to work."

She swallowed hard as his shirt came off and joined her dress. The way the sunlight hit his chest, highlighting the dusting of hair, made her body feel fifty times hotter than a moment before. "I didn't realize you were wearing your swim trunks under your clothes," she said, trying desperately to focus her thoughts.

"I'm not." He unzipped his cargo shorts and let them fall to the ground. Toned, tanned legs disappeared beneath his tight navy blue boxer briefs and her head suddenly spun like she'd had too much to drink. The form-fitting fabric cupped him, showing off the anatomy she'd been trying so hard to forget.

As he strode toward her, she wrenched her gaze from his package, finally looking him in the eyes again. When she did, he cocked an eyebrow.

"What?"

He smirked. "Nothing, sugar. Nothing at all." He grabbed

her hand and pulled her deeper into the lake.

Her body reacted to his term of endearment even as her mind rebelled against it. Heat flooded her system, but not from the sun. His words were like kindling to the desire that smoldered deep in her belly every time he was around.

Icy wetness hit her knees and she squealed again, her mind finally clearing enough to think straight. Submerging sounded like a bad idea, especially since Sawyer was involved. The last thing she wanted to do was be dripping wet and cold to the point of glass-cutting nipples. Wearing her bikini in front of him was bad enough. "I changed my mind. The water is freezing."

"Oh no. You got me in here, you have to come too."

"You're the one who interrupted my solitude then stripped down to your skivvies." Her tone was meant to challenge him, but it didn't seem to be working, as he pulled her in further.

"I didn't think you'd appreciate me skinny dipping, but if you'd prefer, I'd be happy to slip out of these and toss them back on shore." He dropped her hand and reached for the waistband.

As much as she wanted to dare him to do it, she held her ground, refusing to give in to temptation. Being with him again would not make her life easier.

"Let's do it already," she said hastily, trying to dissuade him from taking off his remaining clothing.

"Do it, huh? If you insist."

Before she could object, his arms circled her waist and he pulled her body flush to his. His fingers toyed with the edge of her bikini bottoms as if he might slip beneath the material to cup her naked skin. She gasped as intense pleasure rocketed through her.

"And here I thought you only wanted to go for a swim." His other hand snaked up to the nape of her neck.

"That is what I want. I didn't mean anything else. You're twisting my words again." She pressed her hands to his chest in an effort to put some distance between them, but only succeeded in reminding herself how nice his skin felt under her fingertips. How the crinkly dusting of hair contrasted with the silky smoothness of his hard length, currently pressing against her stomach. Not things she wanted to think about if she was going to stay away from him.

Of course, her position under him had been pretty damn awesome in the hotel room, too.

Stop. It's Sawyer. And fake.

He grinned. A big, know-it-all grin. "Have it your way."

Before she could react, he twisted and flopped backward into the water, taking her with him. Frigid darkness surrounded her as his arms disappeared from her waist. She struggled to the surface, finding her feet and sputtering out water.

"Refreshing, right?" he asked while shaking out his hair as if he were a wet dog.

"Refreshing my ass. What the hell was that for?"

"I told you, inching in doesn't work. You either have to jump off the pier or dive in. Since neither was an option, I opted for a simple dunk."

"You could have warned me."

"True, but then you would've made it harder by trying to resist me." He splashed her and swam away while she swiped water out of her eyes.

Going after him as quickly as she could, she attempted to splash him back, make him drink a little lake water as punishment, but he dodged her. "Jerk," she said, finally giving up so she could catch her breath. Panting, she put her hand to her side, where a stab of pain shot through her.

A second later, Sawyer dived under the water and resurfaced in front of her. Concern creased his forehead. "That's from Tyler's stupid boat ride, isn't it?"

She tilted her head to the side, leveling him with her gaze. "How nice of you to be concerned now when you didn't even think about my well-being when you dunked me."

"You barely even submerged."

"Tell that to my soaking wet hair."

He smoothed a loose strand and secured it behind her ear. "I think it looks pretty good wet." Dropping his hand to her side, he skimmed his fingertips against a large bruise that had bloomed that morning. She'd known she'd bumped the side of the boat, but she hadn't thought she'd bumped it that hard until today. "Does it hurt?"

The tenderness and concern in his voice made it hard to find hers. "Not really. I just look like a total mess."

"You're beautiful."

The conviction of his words settled in her chest, hitching her breath. For a guy who insisted on staying a bachelor, he sure knew the right things to say to a woman. She wrapped her arms protectively around herself. "I'm going to lay out and warm up. I've had enough freezing cold water."

He pulled her back against his chest, the heat from his body instantly quelling her shivers. "I mean it. You're one of the most beautiful women I've ever met, inside and out."

His touch sent a shot of fire through her arms and legs. The desire in her core roared to life. She didn't want to enjoy his words, but damn it, her body wouldn't respect her wishes.

She ached for him deeply, intensely.

"I don't want to be another notch in your bedpost."

"If that's all I wanted, I wouldn't have given you a second glance after our night in the hotel room."

"Yeah, and?"

"And instead I haven't been able to get you out of my mind since. You're the only woman in my thoughts, in my fantasies."

Her legs went limp and she fought to maintain control, but the idea of him having fantasies about her made her yearn to hear all about them, maybe even live them. It didn't matter that her time as his girlfriend would come to an end eventually; all that her tingling girly parts cared about was his attention.

He slid his hand up her side, to the string of her bikini top, his fingers dangerously close to her breast. Memories of the last time he'd touched her flooded her mind and she leaned into him on impulse.

"Yesterday, while I was fixing the roof, I imagined what you might look like in a little swimsuit like this. I have to admit, my imagination didn't nearly do you justice. Real life is so much better. Of course, in my head, this little bit of material spent most of the time crumpled on the ground."

She didn't know what to say. If Sawyer were the real deal, her actual boyfriend instead of a fake one, she'd be putty in his hands. Giving in would surely lead to heartache later on in this situation, but maybe the heartache was worth it.

Every second she spent with Sawyer she was more captivated. He was an amazing businessman, a faithful friend, a considerate roommate, a loyal and heartbroken son, and a caring fake boyfriend.

"I wondered if you would taste the same after being in the lake." He dipped his head and kissed her shoulder while his thumb caressed the side of her breast, slipping under the tiny triangle of material. He licked up to her ear and whispered, "You taste like summer. Did I ever mention, summer is my favorite season?"

Screw it.

She'd done nothing but plan and think about what was coming next, but in turn, she was missing out on the beauty of the moment. And this was a moment she didn't want to miss. Right now, right here, she'd live in the present and give in to the man who'd been tempting her, making her question her dreams for the future, and causing her to yearn for his touch again and again.

Shouldn't she live life? Enjoy all it had to offer? Against her better judgment, she let her head fall to the side, giving him better access. Between the freezing water and his hot mouth on her skin, her nipples were beaded so tightly they hurt. She pressed her hips into him and moaned as his hard length dug into her flesh.

Inching back enough to fit her hand between them, she stroked his length. "I wonder if you taste like summer, too." She found his mouth and kissed him with every ounce of need boiling inside her. He responded, equally eager.

He scooped her into his arms and she wrapped her legs around his waist as he carried her out of the water. Kicking their clothes out of the way, he deposited her on the towel then fished out a condom from his wallet in the pocket of his shorts, and set it on the pile of clothes next to them.

Thank God the man came prepared, because she certainly hadn't. Stopping now that he hovered over her again, wasn't an option she wanted to go with. She wanted Sawyer again, now.

Spreading her legs, she pulled him down on top of her, gasping as his erection pressed against her in just the right place. She squirmed beneath him, begging for more direct contact.

He didn't disappoint. Thrusting his hips, he rubbed the sweet spot between her thighs. Even with material still separating them, he had enough talent to bring her to the edge and push her over it. But before she got anywhere close, he stopped and sat back on his heels.

"What's wrong?" she asked, suddenly panicked. "Is someone coming?" What if his family came looking for them? She would die a million deaths of embarrassment.

"Relax, sugar. The only one coming is you. Well, I will too, eventually." He winked, then slowly untied the strings at her hips, as if he were unwrapping a delicate package. His expression of eager anticipation made her giggle. "Something funny?"

Her response turned into a moan in her throat when his tongue swept across her newly exposed skin, sending her head spinning. The laughter vanished, replaced by deep breaths and shaky gasps. Every flick and swirl of his tongue on her needy flesh was like a shot of electricity through her body. She rocked her hips, keeping pace with his movements, intensifying each one until she felt as if her body was about to explode like a firework. When he finally moved up her body to her breasts, she quivered with aftershocks.

Sunlight warmed her breasts as he pushed the tiny triangles of material to the side. His teeth nipped at her tight buds, sending another round of shockwaves through her body. She wiggled her hips against him, begging him for more.

Grabbing the foil packet, he sheathed himself and inched into her, achingly slow.

She expected him to feel cold from the lake, but instead he was hot and hard and huge moving inside her. Wrapping her legs around him, she thrust her hips, taking him deeper. He groaned and picked up his pace, kissing her neck and nibbling her collarbone.

She stopped him long enough to make him roll over onto his back, and then she climbed on top, straddling his hips. Slowly lowering her body, she took every inch of him, moaning as he hit the spot inside that made her tremble. His hands slid up her thighs until they reached her heat, rubbing circles against her skin.

Clinging to him with every thrust, she called out his name as waves of pleasure crashed over her like the tide on a stormy sea. He responded, pulling her down onto his chest, covering her mouth with his, claiming her.

In that moment, she was his, and she'd never felt more complete.

Chapter Sixteen

Sawyer squinted up into the bright sky. A few puffball clouds drifted past, casting shadows on the ground and providing a minute or two of shade for their sun-kissed bodies. He really should have put on sunscreen earlier, but given his current situation, with Olivia's body tucked into his side, he really couldn't complain. Sunburn was a tiny, insignificant price to pay to have this afternoon with her, alone and naked, on the beach at the cabin.

Maybe it was the afterglow of sex talking, or maybe it was simply something she did to him, but regardless, he hadn't been this content and happy in a long time.

She made him want to change. With her around, he wanted to slow down, take it easy. He still cared about the future of his company, but she had a way of making him forget about it for a few minutes and see that other things were important too.

He finally understood the future she wanted to have

someday. Being with someone like Olivia, having a home like the cabin, being successful at work—he got why she wanted all of that now that she was back. Part of him wished he could be the one to give it all to her. She'd done so much for him, with the cabin and work and during their fake relationship. Too bad he couldn't offer her more than housing and a job reference. She deserved better than that…better than him.

"My dad and I used to come here all the time. It was our little oasis."

She propped herself up on an elbow beside him, her hand resting on his chest over his heart. He wondered if she could feel it beating, calm and steady, beneath her palm. "What did you guys do here?"

"While everyone else was still asleep, we'd dig up worms and grab our poles and be out on the lake as the sun was cresting that ridge." He pointed off into the distance. It probably looked like any other hill, but to him it was a reminder of all the things he'd lost. The thought that he might have to add the cabin to that list worried him.

"I bet you miss it."

"I do. That's our—well, my—little boat over there. I haven't been out in a long time. Too busy with work to give up an entire weekend and come here. Sunday dinner is about as much as I have time for. Sterling Enterprises isn't going to save itself."

"It doesn't need to. You're going to land the Marcus project, I know it."

Hearing her confidence in his abilities made his chest tighten. He'd never taken so much pride in his work as he did in that moment.

It also made him realize how his work got in the way of so many other aspects of his life, and made him wish there was a better way to balance it all. As it was, he couldn't stop feeling like he was doing a piss poor job of living. Like she said, he needed to take better care of himself, and exist for more than work, the bar, and soccer.

How the hell did Olivia know him so well? Didn't he feel better today, here with her, not working, than he had in months? Wasn't that true the other times she'd been at his side, even while they poured over Marcus project notes, or carpooled to work, or ate Chinese takeout straight from the container?

He rolled to his side, facing her. The bruise on her ribs was another reminder of how he put the wrong things first. "I wish I'd been the one to offer to grab the power washer for Gramps, then I would've taken you out on the boat and you wouldn't have gotten hurt."

It took him a good minute of staring off into the distance before he finally met her gaze and cleared his throat. "When I heard you scream, all I could think was that it was happening again. I was losing someone to the lake."

Cupping his jaw, she peered into his eyes. "No one should have to live through what you have."

He drew circles on her skin as he spoke. "It took me back to when my parents died. I could barely think straight. I could've killed Tyler for joyriding with you."

She smiled, her eyes twinkling. "Careful, Sawyer. I might start thinking you care about me on a deeper level. That would be bad for your whole carefree-bachelor persona." Hopping to her feet, she pulled on her sundress and slipped into her sandals. "Come on. We should head back. We can't hang out here all afternoon. Your family might get the wrong idea about us."

"What? Like we're a couple, sneaking off to fool around?" Didn't sound as terrible as he once thought it would. Did it sound terrible to her?

"Exactly."

He put on his clothes over his now mostly dry boxer briefs, taking his time as he pulled himself back together. The term *couple* used to send a chill up his spine, but now it didn't bother him. Of course, Olivia wouldn't look at them as a couple because she wanted a relationship with someone who could offer her a real future. He still didn't feel like the guy to give that to her.

So why did he suddenly feel like this thing with Olivia was more than a hookup hoax?

. . .

Walking the path back to the cabin, Olivia heard talking up ahead, though she couldn't make out the voice. "Who's that?" she whispered.

Sawyer paused, listening.

The person spoke again. "I'll need to make a few improvements over the winter, but mostly cosmetic stuff."

"It's Tyler." Sawyer inched forward.

"I'd like to have it on the market by spring. I'm ready to unload it." Tyler laughed at something they couldn't hear, obviously talking on his cell. "Yeah, sounds good. Let me know what the other cabins sell for this summer and what amenities they have. I want top dollar for this place with minimal work."

When he hung up and started back toward the cabin, Sawyer blocked his path. "What the hell was that about? Are you planning on selling the cabin?" Sawyer's voice sounded barely controlled. She didn't blame him at all. Why would anyone work so hard to win the deed only to sell it?

"It'll be my cabin by then, and yeah, I am."

"Why would you do that?"

Tyler looked away, fumbling as he tried to shove his phone back into his pocket.

"Tell me. Why work so hard to get the cabin and then sell it?"

"A little extra money—or a lot, according to my realtor—could go a long way to making life more comfortable with the new baby." He met his gaze for a minute before looking out to the lake. "Things haven't been stable at work, and with the house and new SUV payments…"

"You could get a second job. Or ask for help. You don't need to go so far as to swindle the cabin out of the family and sell it."

"You should talk. If you're such an honorable grandson, then what the hell is she doing here?" Tyler sneered viciously.

She took a step toward Sawyer's side. Something about the way Tyler always looked at her gave her the creeps.

"You will not speak to my girlfriend like that. She's here because I invited her here, and in case you haven't noticed yet, Gran is thrilled to have her. Think Gran will be thrilled to hear your plan to sell the cabin?"

Tyler shrugged. "Think Gran will be happy to hear Olivia's some girl you're using to win?"

Olivia held her breath and peered up at Sawyer. How the hell did Tyler know the truth? They'd been in character and convincing as a couple this whole time, hadn't they?

Sawyer laughed easily, as if Tyler's accusations meant nothing. "I don't know where you got that crazy idea, but it's not true."

She bit her lip, looking at the ground. Hearing him say the words, talk about their relationship, made it feel so real, almost as real as her feelings a few minutes ago, when he'd been inside of her and the world around them had disappeared into a haze of lust and love.

Her chest constricted. Did she love him?

Being with him was beyond anything she'd hoped to find in the person she'd spend the rest of her life with, but he was more than that. Every time he let her in a little bit deeper, shared more about his parents, hearing the pain in his voice when he thought she was in danger on the lake…it seeped into her soul, joining them on a primal level. Sure, they made sparks fly in the sack, but never had she experienced this feeling of absolute connectivity with a man. Sawyer had quickly become a part of her entire essence.

He'd claimed her heart.

Tyler puffed up his chest defensively. "On the boat, Olivia was talking to herself about some kind of plan and deal. It didn't take me long to put it all together. The coincidence of your sudden relationship, and them signing over the cabin, she was in the right place at the right time, wasn't she?"

Had she mentioned the plan when she was scared out of her mind on the boat? No. Maybe?

Sawyer's jaw visibly clenched.

"Do you really think we'd be sleeping together if we weren't a couple?" Olivia asked. "Our feelings for each other are…"

Sawyer continued when she trailed off. "Our feelings are real."

"I love him and I don't care what you think you heard," she added quickly and without thought.

Oh shit. I said that out loud.

Sawyer shot her a questioning look.

"What's Olivia's middle name?" Tyler asked.

Sawyer swore under his breath. They were caught.

"I knew it," Tyler said.

Defending their relationship to the rest of the family wasn't on her to-do list for the day, not when she was confused about what her feelings really were. Did she love him? Did she simply love having someone like him around? Was the hookup lust clouding her brain and toying with her emotions?

"They've always valued loyalty to family over anything else," Sawyer said. "Regardless of my relationship status, I'll keep this cabin in the family forever. If I never have my own children, I'll give it to someone who deserves it, someone who's blood. Can you say that?"

"Telling them we're both lying only makes it more likely they'll decide not to give it to either of us. I'm not willing to risk an outsider getting this place. I'll keep quiet if you will."

"Okay, but if you or Sophia so much as whisper a hint about this to anyone, our deal is off." Sawyer pulled her by the hand toward the house. He didn't stop until they were back in their room with the doors and windows closed.

Gripping her shoulders, he stared at her as if he were trying to see directly into her soul. "Did you mean what you said back there? Do you…" He paused, searching her eyes for the truth while his hands slid up her neck and into her hair. "Do you love me?"

She did *not* love him. She was only caught up in their act and making more out of the connection she felt with him. That's all. Sure. She wanted to look away but couldn't. Did she love him? She didn't know. The thought of their charade ending soon didn't sit well in her. But did she actually *love* him?

A raw pain erupted in her chest. She did.

But it didn't matter. He was a sworn bachelor. He would never love her back. Time and time again, she'd mistaken his fake feelings for real ones, only to have him laugh off their situation. Could she handle it if he laughed off her love for him, too? Nope. She couldn't deal with that kind of whole-hearted rejection again.

"Apparently my acting skills are improving," she laughed nervously, hoping he bought her lie.

Something that looked a lot like pain flashed through his eyes as his shoulders drooped. For a second she expected him to start yelling, but then he chuckled and nudged her arm playfully.

"I knew you'd be a great partner in this scam. Impressive." Without another word, he walked out of the room.

Chapter Seventeen

Olivia smiled at the woman next to her on the couch at Tyler and Sophia's house, already having forgotten her name. Mildred? Margaret? It didn't matter either way. She was on Sophia's side of the family and therefore someone she probably would never have to see again.

Regardless, she smiled sweetly and spoke kindly, listening intently as the woman droned on about pregnancy symptoms and how hers compared to Sophia's. She tried her best to look interested in swollen ankles, morning sickness, and strange food cravings but it was challenging. Someday, if she was lucky, she would be able to contribute her own stories, but that was in the distant future.

Sawyer sat on her other side, his arm casually thrown across the back of the couch, near enough to her shoulders that anyone looking would think they were cuddling, even though they weren't actually touching. She preferred it that way.

Since the day on the beach, they hadn't spoken about what had happened, or what was said between them, and she was okay with that. She didn't want to deal with the realization of how she felt about him anyway. So instead, they pretended it hadn't happened.

He'd been too focused on presenting to Marcus to deal with any lingering questions about their weekend at the cabin anyway. With every day that passed, Sawyer looked a little worse. If they didn't hear something soon, she was starting to worry he'd really follow in his father's footsteps and drop dead of a heart attack.

She had to admit, the stress had been bothering her too. Restless nights and weird dreams were making her long for the days when she used to be able to sleep in. Even her appetite was off. Nothing except fruit looked appealing anymore and her stomach had bordered on nauseated for the last week or so. She did not deal with stress well.

The baby shower hadn't spurred much excitement from Sawyer, but she thought it would be a great distraction, at least for a day. Now that they were here, she was right. He'd been joking and visiting with everyone, seemingly happier than she'd seen him in weeks. Even she felt in better spirits socializing.

"Let's head outside," he said. "There are people I want to introduce you to."

She accepted his hand and followed him out to the deck off the side of the house. A warm summer breeze blew through her hair as they wandered over to a couple leaning against the railing.

"Aunt Bea and Uncle Stan, this is my girlfriend Olivia," Sawyer said, motioning to the older couple. "They're in town from Santa Anna."

"Nice to meet you," she said, smiling while trying to commit their names and faces to memory. These were definitely people who could show up again at Gran and Gramps birthday party. A girlfriend would remember their names.

"Finally, a girl who is ballsy enough to hook you. I like you already," Stan said, grinning ear to ear. "You must be a feisty one."

"I do my best to keep him in line." She glanced at Sawyer to gauge his reaction. He looked genuinely amused and not at all put off by the suggestion of being tied down.

"You have no idea." He grinned and pulled her against his side. She snuggled into him, playing along. It wasn't a hardship since his arms always made her feel protected and loved. She stiffened slightly, forcing the notion of love from her mind, not ready to go there again.

When there was a lull in conversation, she asked, "How long are you staying in town? Maybe we can have dinner one night. At our place."

Our place. The ease of saying it surprised her.

"Just the weekend," Stan said. "We'd hoped to stay longer this time, but a friend of ours has landed himself in the hospital and we've got to get back to take care of his house and pets."

Bea looped her arm through Stan's. "If you'll excuse us, we still haven't had a chance to say hello to Gran." They wandered back into the house.

The deck overlooked the rolling hills of the Hudson Valley—green for as far as they could see, dotted with houses here and there. She understood a little more why Tyler didn't feel the need to keep the cabin. With this view, he probably felt like he was on vacation every time he was out there.

Sawyer's fingers traced a path back and forth across her lower back as they stood there enjoying the beautiful scenery and the sun setting over the hills. Not so long ago, feeling his hand there would have made her uncomfortable, but lately, it seemed to bring her peace. Her nervousness at having to meet new family and friends melted away and she simply embraced the moment of calm. Sighing, she threaded her arm around his waist and relaxed.

The sun dipped lower and lower on the horizon, casting the trees into warm amber light. Fireflies glowed as dusk set around them and she giggled when one lit up an inch from her face, startling her.

"Scared of a little lightning bug? Sad."

She swatted him on the chest. "I didn't expect it to be so close to my face."

"Maybe he likes your face. Maybe he thinks you're pretty foxy. Isn't that why they light up to begin with? To attract the opposite sex?" He grinned down at her.

All this talk about sex and attraction stirred up those feelings for him she was trying so hard to ignore. She shrugged. "How would I know? I'm not an expert on the sexuality of bugs."

"Your expertise is reserved solely for humans, huh? Good to know."

"You know what I meant." She hit him again. Her hand lingered on his chest. She hadn't had this much contact with him in a week and it felt good. Really good.

"I suppose we should stop watching the view and actually visit with some of the other guests, huh? I wonder who else is out here..." His voice trailed off as they looked around the deck, which had been bustling with activity earlier, but was now desolate.

This whole time they'd been cuddling each other and no one had even been around to see. How had they not noticed everyone else leaving? Usually they were both so on their guard at these family functions that they noted each person's every move.

As if reaching the same conclusion simultaneously, they both dropped their arms and stepped away from each other. His brow creased as he held her gaze. A sense of disbelief and confusion radiated off of him, matching her feelings exactly.

Turning, they made their way back into the house without another word.

. . .

Sawyer sipped another mouthful of sangria and tried not to show how much he disliked it. Of course there was also soda and water, but he needed alcohol to get through the rest of the evening. Getting so close and cuddly with Olivia earlier, without even meaning to, had really thrown him for a loop. It was as if he'd lost time when he was out on the deck with her. The idea he could be so comfortable with someone that he'd simply lose all sense of time and place made his heart race.

What would make him so focused on her that he forgot everything else around him? That he'd forget they were acting, and simply enjoy the moment without thought of what people would expect of them?

"Hey, earth to Sawyer," Tyler said, snapping his fingers.

"It's your turn, dude."

He looked around feeling lost. "Um…"

"*Baby Got Back*," Olivia whispered. "Say it."

"*Baby Got Back,*" he said.

Everyone laughed.

"Guess we know what's on his mind," Uncle Stan said.

The game moved on to his left and he turned to whisper to Olivia. "What was that?"

"The name of a song with baby in the title. It looked like you needed help, and apparently you did, if you didn't even know what game we're playing."

"And you couldn't have told me to say one a little less… suggestive?"

She giggled. "It was the only other one I could think of and I didn't want to say it. So I gave it to you."

"Thanks, I think." He sighed and sunk further into the couch.

"I could have left you floundering and then you'd have to face your punishment like the big baby you're acting like."

"And what would my punishment have been?" If it was a spanking, he was all in. The next game, he'd be the worst player in the history of baby showers.

She nodded toward the people sucking apple juice out of baby bottles, each looking more exhausted than the last.

"Okay, thank you. That would be humiliating."

As the games continued, he and Olivia continued to be terrible at each one. Of course, she was marginally better than him. When she'd had to diaper the toy baby, she'd come in third, whereas he'd come in last. And when he'd picked up the doll to show off his handiwork, the damn diaper had fallen straight to the floor. Even he'd had to laugh at that one.

But when Olivia cradled the doll in her arms while waiting for the next game to begin, a lump formed in his throat, and no amount of sangria had been able to dislodge it. She looked amazing holding a baby, even a toy one. He glanced to Tyler and Sophia, who had moved on to opening gifts. His cousin held up a tiny baseball jersey and he was sure there was a twinkle of moisture in the soon-to-be father's eyes.

Olivia cooed. "So sweet."

Yes, she is, he thought, his attention returning to the woman at his side. She was the sweetest thing he'd had the pleasure of experiencing. She was a woman unlike any other.

The spike of jealousy toward his cousin's life unsettled him. But the jolt of longing for a life like that with Olivia nearly made him see stars. Was it possible he could actually imagine a future with her? What kind of future could he honestly commit to?

He drained his glass of sangria and hoped that if he ate enough of the alcohol soaked fruit, he'd find the answers he needed.

• • •

Olivia sat on the crinkly white paper covering the examining table in the doctor's office and waited impatiently. She had so many other things to do. Taking time off work for him to tell her she had the flu, or needed more sleep, was not one of them, but on the off chance that her continued tiredness and lack of appetite was something serious, she'd wait and see what he had to say. She was ready to feel better.

The doctor walked in and went straight to the counter, opening her chart. He glanced quickly to the test strip laying across the container of urine the nurse had made her supply and noted something on her paperwork.

"So, am I dying?" she asked, mostly joking.

"No. You're pregnant." The doctor turned to face her, leaning against the counter.

"I'm what now?"

"When was your last period?"

The room tilted and she clung to the edges of the table. Her last period? A couple of weeks before the gala?

"Six weeks ago or so." She felt faint as the words left her mouth. She was late. She was never late.

"It looks like you haven't had a prescription for birth control refilled since…" He flipped back in her chart. "Years. Is there a reason you stopped taking them?"

"I took my pills religiously until I ran out. It was hard to get them in some countries while traveling. I meant to come in and get a new prescription when I got home, but I've been so busy…"

How could she be so stupid not to take precautions? But Sawyer had.

"Both times Sawyer used a condom. I saw him put the damn thing on." She hopped off the table and paced. "This doesn't make any sense."

"Are you sure he put it on correctly? He used a new one every time?"

"Yes and gross. How many ways are there to put on a condom? Is it even possible to do it wrong?"

"You'd be amazed at some of the things I've heard. Regardless, condoms are not one hundred percent effective even if used correctly. That's why doctors always recommend a secondary contraception as well, like the pill."

"Thanks for rubbing it in, doc." She scowled at him. "But wouldn't we notice its *ineffectiveness* in some way? Leakage or something?" Just saying the words made her stomach do another flip-flop.

"Not necessarily."

"But I can't be…"

The doctor pulled a chair closer to the side of the bed. "There are options, if you'd like to discuss them."

"Options?" She'd always planned to have children at some point. The only option in her mind was whether or not she'd ask for an epidural during labor. There was no way she was giving up this baby. "No. I want my baby."

"Okay then. Congratulations are in order. Start taking pre-natal vitamins once a day and make an appointment with your obstetrician."

With that, he left the room, the door closing behind him with a soft thud.

A baby?

A baby.

I'm having a baby. Sawyer's baby.

Chapter Eighteen

Sawyer paced his office. Marcus had called to request a meeting at two and it was already almost three. This had to be it. A couple of weeks had passed since their final presentation, which was more than enough time for him to decide who he wanted on the project. It had to be a meeting to say he'd chosen Sterling, but he hoped the day would go even better than that.

After he dealt with Marcus, he was taking Olivia out to celebrate. While they were at dinner—he'd already made a reservation at one of the nicest places in town—he planned to offer her something he'd never expected.

A future with him. If she'd have him.

He'd made her a position at Sterling. It wasn't a top spot or anything, but higher than her current one. It would also be full-time and permanent.

More than that, he wanted to offer her a real relationship—not that he'd gone so far as to buy a ring or anything.

He was miles away from being there yet, if ever, but he didn't want to stop dating her either. Bachelorhood be damned, he liked her, and the thought of going back to flirting with random women at the bar didn't thrill him. He owed it to himself, and her, to see if there was anything real between them.

It wasn't the lifelong commitment she wanted, but it was all he could offer.

"Do you have a minute?" Olivia asked, coming to his door.

He glanced at his watch again. He didn't have time but he didn't want to brush her off just because he was anxious. "Sure. Come in."

She closed the door, leaning against it. The shadows under her eyes looked darker and the whites of her eyes had a pink tinge. Had she been crying?

"Are you okay?"

She nodded. "Yes and no. I…" She bit her lip and looked at the floor. Her hand went to the door handle as if she wanted to leave. "I should do this at the apartment, not here. I don't know what I was thinking."

He went to her, grasping her shoulders and peering at her. "Tell me."

"This isn't the right time or place, but you should know as soon as possible." She met his gaze and fresh tears lined her lower lids.

"What? Whatever it is, it'll be okay."

"I went to the doctor today." She bit her lip.

"Are you sick?" She didn't look as great as she usually did, but she didn't really look sick either.

"I'm…pregnant."

He dropped his hands to his sides and stepped back until

he hit his desk. Perching on the edge, he felt the room spin. What did she say? No. It wasn't possible. He could barely manage a dating commitment. He couldn't handle having a baby with someone.

"But we...but you're on...and I used..."

"I'm not on any pills," she whispered. "I forgot to get a prescription when I came back to the States."

"You forgot?" his voice rose an octave.

"I haven't taken them in years. I forgot to start up again." She folded her arms across her chest. "User error can contribute to condoms being less effective. Didn't *you* know *that*?"

"If I'd known that, I wouldn't have bothered using one, for all the damn good it did! And there was no 'user error' on my part. I've never had this happen any other time I've had sex."

"We weren't even supposed to have sex!"

"You wanted it as much as I did. I definitely didn't hear you complaining." Olivia swiped at the tears running down her cheeks, and his chest felt as if it would cave in. "I'm sorry," he said. "I shouldn't have yelled. This wasn't the news I expected today."

"Tell me about it," she mumbled. "I thought you should know as soon as I did, since this baby is as much yours as it is mine."

His baby. Their baby.

He'd wanted to keep their relationship going, but a baby? He tried to focus his thoughts. "But I can't. I never wanted kids."

"Of course you don't. What bachelor would?" Olivia's chin quivered as she clearly tried to hold back another round of tears.

His chest constricted again. This wasn't what he wanted. He wanted a normal dating relationship with her, not a baby. But he didn't want to hurt her. Damn it, why couldn't he have a little time to deal with his thoughts before having to talk rationally about this?

"I didn't mean…"

"I know what you meant. You've made it clear the whole time. You don't do commitment. You don't do relationships. I don't even know why I bothered telling you." She bit her lip as tears continued to slip down her cheeks. She swept at them quickly. "I can't believe I did this to myself again. I thought I learned my lesson after Sam, but apparently not."

"I'm nothing like Sam," he said forcefully. He would never dump her or hurt her that way. "I would never get engaged to you like that."

Olivia sucked in a breath and staggered back a step.

Shit. That came out all wrong.

Sawyer ran his hands through his hair. "I just need time to think. To—"

There was a knock at the door and she turned to answer it.

"He's here, Mr. Sterling," said Candace. Her gaze darted between Sawyer and Olivia, sizing up the situation and obviously realizing this wasn't an average business meeting. She probably thought they were having a lover's spat.

Ha. I wish.

"Should I send him in?" she asked.

"Yes, of course. Let's not keep him waiting." Sawyer took a deep breath. "We'll talk more at home, okay?"

Home. Where his fake girlfriend and real baby-to-be would be waiting for him. A chill ran down his spine. He could barely be a boyfriend and now he was supposed to be a father?

The thought of having someone who depended on him the way a child would sent fear—deep, primal, all encompassing fear—through his body. This was his worst nightmare. He wanted to follow in his father's footsteps with the company, but he'd never planned to go so far as to have a child to leave behind when his own ticket came up.

What the hell was he going to do?

He thought he saw Olivia nod before she slipped out of his office. Hopefully by the time he got home, he'd be able to think clearly and figure out how they were going to deal with having a baby together. The idea of a baby made his chest hurt. Taking a deep breath, he forced his thoughts off of his personal life and onto the task at hand. Marcus.

He pulled his shoulders back, straightened his tie, and plastered a confident smile on his face. This was it. The moment of truth. Everything else would have to wait.

He extended his hand as Marcus walked into his office. "Nice to see you again." Marcus's handshake was firm, but his demeanor was relaxed. "Since you called this meeting, I'll let you have the floor," Sawyer said.

"I liked what I saw in your presentation, and I like the way you guys think around here. I'd like to sign the contract with you."

Sawyer shook Marcus's hand again, overjoyed and relieved. "Thank you. You won't regret it."

"On one condition," Marcus stated flatly.

"Name it."

"I need you to physically oversee the marketing campaign. There are communication barriers I'm not sure we can break via email. I need you there, at least to get them kicked off on each campaign."

Time away? But he'd been planning on starting a real relationship with Olivia. Of course, that was before all this talk of a baby. He wasn't cut out to be a father. His own, as much as he loved him, had been a workaholic and Sawyer was already fulfilling that role. That's what he knew how to be. That's what he was good at. How was he supposed to suddenly tap into some paternal instincts he wasn't even sure he had?

This wasn't ideal, not when he knew Olivia wanted a stable commitment. Not with a baby on the way. Before, there'd been a chance she might be content with dating, but now? Now she would want more. Did he?

"How long do you think I'd be needed overseas? If it's to get things started in each region, are we talking a week in each place? More? Less?"

"We're not sure. Our vision has to be communicated properly. Could be a few months by the time you're done. Of course, your expenses will be paid in full."

"Can we do it remotely, via satellite video conferencing?"

Marcus shrugged. "Depends on the region. It's possible, but I wouldn't count on it. I need your agreement on this before I sign. If you don't think you can commit, then now's the time to tell me."

Why did everything have to be a commitment?

Those days of freedom were gone and if he didn't embrace this opportunity with Marcus now, he'd lose it. He'd explain everything to Olivia tonight. As an added benefit, time away would give him a chance to sort out his feelings about the baby, about being a father—something he couldn't even begin to wrap his head around right now.

"I'll make it happen. I'm thrilled you picked Sterling."

"Good. Rally the troops and let's tell them all the good news."

Sawyer blanched. "Now?"

"Why not? Let's make it official."

Sawyer lifted the phone receiver to his ear. "Candace, call everyone over. I have an important announcement."

Through the blinds he spotted Olivia trying to look busy, even though he could tell she was doing anything but work. He wished he could tell her about the required travel in private.

Moments later, a group had formed outside of his office. With little time for any other options, he led the way across the room, but not before catching Olivia's gaze and winking. He hoped she knew it meant everything would be okay.

Together, he and Marcus went to the small raised area at one end of the room, where they would sometimes do big company presentations. Once on the little stage, he raised his hands and the excited chatter dissipated.

"Thank you all for gathering so quickly." He paused, trying to organize his thoughts. There were too many things swirling around in his brain today. "I have the great honor of announcing Todd Marcus has decided to sign with Sterling!"

Applause thundered through the room. Pride swelled within him. He'd done it. Months of hard work finally paid off. Hopefully this would be the start of a long and prosperous partnership with Marcus.

He searched for Olivia in the crowd, finally finding her in the center of the room, cheering along with everyone. Even with everything going on in her life, she was happy for him, for the company she was a temporary employee at. She was amazing.

"Let them hear the rest." Marcus nudged him to continue.

Sawyer held up his hands and the crowd quieted. "There's more. Also exciting, I think, though unexpected. Marcus has asked me to supervise the marketing efforts in each region to make sure the vision we created is maintained and communicated. I won't be gone long, but it could be a few months."

Sawyer looked back to Olivia, but she wasn't where she had been. Scanning the crowd, he finally spotted her by the bank of elevators. Even at a distance, he saw her shoulders shake and her eyes glistening with new tears. He knew she'd be upset—about the travel, about the baby. Everything.

A strong hand gripped his shoulder as he started walking toward her.

"Let's celebrate. I've made reservations at Bernie's," Marcus said.

Olivia stepped into the elevator, meeting his gaze briefly before the door closed. It was enough time to see the hurt and accusation on her face.

His insides twisted and he wanted more than anything to go after her, but Marcus squeezed his shoulder again looking for an answer. Reluctantly, he plastered a celebration-worthy smile on his face. He had to push everything else aside and finalize this contract. Then he'd go back to his apartment and deal with Olivia and the baby situation, and maybe he'd figure out what the hell he would do about it all.

• • •

Blinking away yet another rush of tears, Olivia jammed clothes into her bag. Being out of Sawyer's apartment by the time he strolled back home was a necessity.

She couldn't look at him and know that everything she'd thought he'd felt for her was nothing more than the lie they'd set out to tell together. He'd done his part. He'd played along as her boyfriend, showing her off, kissing her, cuddling her...*more...*

She had no one to blame but herself for the feelings she'd developed for him. He'd been truthful from the start about what he wanted: the cabin to call his home, a temporary girlfriend, and no real commitment. And then she'd gotten pregnant. So much for commitment free. But there had been moments when she'd thought maybe he might want more, too. Obviously those moments were a product of wishful thinking.

Since college and her relationship with Sam, the only thing she'd wanted was stability, a partner in life, and a family. Sam had been the first to rip that dream away from her and she'd fled from him, from her failure, from everything she hoped for but wouldn't have. For five years, she'd travelled the world to escape her feelings about the past.

Now it was Sawyer's turn to reject her and ruin everything. Heartache triggered the same fight or flight response, but this time she couldn't run away, not when there was a child growing inside of her. This time, she had no choice but to stay and face her mistakes.

She'd gone into this arrangement knowing it was just that...a business arrangement, not a serious relationship. Wasn't this exactly what they'd both wanted—an end date so they could move on with the rest of their lives? Maybe it's what she'd convinced herself she wanted. But that was before there was a baby involved.

He'd said he wasn't father material, that he never wanted children. It looked like he was proving his point by agreeing to travel, which would take him away from his responsibilities, away from his son or daughter…away from her.

Overcome by the pain radiating through her chest, Olivia sank to the floor and leaned against the bed. Tears rolled down her already blotchy cheeks. As much as she'd tried to deny it, as much as she didn't want it to be true, she couldn't ignore the facts any longer.

She'd fallen for Sawyer.

Fake boyfriend or not, baby or no baby, she'd given him her heart, her soul, her everything. He was supposed to be a placeholder so she could get her life settled before finding the love of her life. Instead, she'd fallen for the playboy, the man who never wanted a future with any woman, let alone her.

How had she been so stupid again?

Aidan had warned her not to get too close, and she'd ignored him, believing she was strong enough to handle Sawyer. But she wasn't. He'd become her whole world and now he'd agreed to leave it without so much as warning her first. He didn't care about her, or their relationship. He didn't care about their child.

How was she going to continue this charade for another few weeks?

She wasn't, that's how.

Screw him. Screw his stupid cabin and his deceitful plan. If he could make choices for his future without even considering her feelings, then so could she. Starting right now.

Pulling herself from the floor, she grabbed the last of her things, took one more look around the room she'd enjoyed for the last two months, and closed the door—leaving Sawyer in the past along with the rest of her dreams and hopes for the future with him.

She was back to having no apartment, and after she called the human resources department tomorrow and quit, she'd have no job either. The last two months of hard work, gone with a positive pregnancy test. But she had the baby, and regardless of how Sawyer felt about being a dad, she was ready and excited to be a mother—even a single mother.

Maybe her future wasn't exactly as she hoped, but she would do whatever it took to make a good life for her child. With or without Sawyer by her side.

After a long, snot-filled taxi ride, she used the key her brother had given her to his apartment. Seeing him and admitting what she'd done was the last thing she wanted to do, but she had nowhere else to turn.

Grabbing the extra blanket and pillow from the closet, she curled up on the couch and gave into the pain, hoping by the time Aidan got home from work, she'd be ready to take his lecture. She didn't want to hear it, but she certainly deserved it.

Chapter Nineteen

"Olivia!" Sawyer threw open the door to the apartment. It was late. He'd been forced to celebrate with Marcus and the rest of the team for the better part of the evening, much later than he'd anticipated or wanted. He strode down the hall toward her bedroom and knocked on her door. "You in there?"

Silence.

Pounding on the door, he called out again, louder. "Talk to me." The breath caught in his throat as he waited for her response.

Again, silence.

Twisting the knob, he inched the door open and peered inside.

Her room was as vacant as the rest of the apartment. Empty hangers littered the closet. Her dresser drawers were picked clean. The bathroom vanity confirmed his fears— Olivia was gone.

He'd known she'd be upset with him over the travel, and especially his reaction to the baby, but he'd never expected her to move out. He pulled his cell phone from his pocket and dialed her number, then sat on the edge of her bed, waiting for her to pick up. When she didn't, he left a quick message to call him back, that he was sorry, and he wanted to talk.

Flopping onto her pillow, he breathed deep, taking in her scent, still lingering on the fabric. God, he loved the way she smelled, like sunshine and vanilla.

He'd been working so hard for so long for the success he'd achieved today and now the only person he really wanted to celebrate with had moved out and wasn't taking his calls.

He dialed her again, leaving a more urgent message when she still didn't pick up. After the sixth message, he had to restrain himself from throwing his phone across the room. Instead, he dialed Aidan.

"I warned you not to hurt her like you did Tammy," Aidan said, in a tone so eerily soft that it told Sawyer he was pissed and barely keeping it together.

He sighed with relief. "Good. Then you've spoken to Olivia."

"I'd sound a little less excited, if I were you."

"Where is she?" If she was at Aidan's, he was going over there immediately.

"I found her curled up on my couch with a mess of used tissues littering my floor. What did you do to my sister?"

"Nothing. It's a misunderstanding. I'll come over and explain."

"No."

"No what?"

"You won't step foot inside this apartment until I talk to her."

His blood pressure spiked with his anger. This had nothing to do with Aidan and he had no right to play gatekeeper. "This is between me and her. Not you." He practically growled the last few words before hanging up.

She might be Aidan's sister, but she was his girlfriend. Fake girlfriend. Whatever.

She was his. He just had to win her back.

· · ·

"Wake up."

Olivia stirred and batted at whatever was making noise. Her head thumped to the beat of her pulse and her eyes felt as if she'd walked through a sandstorm. Pulling the blanket up around her ear, she attempted to block out the rest of the world. She wanted to stay tucked away in her cocoon forever.

"He's on his way over, so you better tell me what happened."

She groaned. The thought of admitting the pain and rejection to her brother, his best friend, made her nauseated. Or maybe that was pregnancy hormones.

Aidan had been right. Sawyer was bad news from the start, but she didn't listen and now she was a giant ball of snot and sore eyes with a big old broken heart dying in her chest. Not that she was being "overly dramatic," as Sawyer would say.

Tears welled in her eyes at the memory of him teasing

her, calling her out on her behavior. He simultaneous annoyed and amused her every time. She'd miss that part of their relationship.

Fake relationship.

She pushed herself to a sitting position and met her brother's gaze. Anger and protectiveness hardened his features.

"What happened?"

She sighed, feeling defeat throughout her entire body. "He got the Marcus project."

"But that's a good thing."

She chuckled. "I used to think so, too. It still is, I guess." She didn't want to admit her feelings to her brother, or Sawyer, or anyone else. If she said them out loud, then they were out there in the world. If she kept them to herself, maybe she could convince herself they didn't exist.

"And?"

She chewed the inside of her cheek. "And Marcus wants him to travel, to kick off the marketing teams in each region so nothing about their brand message is lost in translation."

"That's bad why?"

"Because he didn't tell me it was part of the deal. Because he didn't even once consider I might care he was going away. Because I fell for him, okay?" A sob bubbled up as the pain in her chest reared up again. "Because…I'm pregnant."

Aidan's arms were around her in seconds, cradling her to his chest, rubbing her back while she sobbed. When her cries turned to stuttered breaths, he called down to the doorman, barring Sawyer from the building.

"I should've listened to you. I should've known better than to get involved with a guy like him. I never meant to put myself through this again. But, he was just so…"

"He's just so dead," Aidan said flatly.

• • •

Sawyer stretched out his hamstrings, groaning with the tension in his muscles. It was as if his body was rejecting him, too.

A stab of pain pierced his chest for about the hundredth time. Maybe he was already in the thousands. He'd lost count somewhere around last Tuesday. Now he was numb most of the time.

Focus. Stretch. Kick the ball. Kick some ass.

Then go home. Alone.

He pushed the negative thoughts from his mind as much as he could. They were still there, always there, lingering in the shadows, haunting his dreams.

If he'd known back when this whole thing started that his life would end up a mess, vacant and void where it used to be full, he wondered if he'd still make the choice to get involved with Olivia. During the day he'd been able to keep busy and convince himself that no, given the choice, he wouldn't go through this again. No woman was worth it. This experience with Olivia proved how much hurt came from relationships. At night, however, when he couldn't keep himself distracted by work, she consumed his thoughts. His missed her scent, her laugh, her sarcastic teasing. He missed the tenderness in her eyes, the heat in her caress, and the passion in her kisses.

"What the hell are you doing here?" Aidan asked.

"Yoga. What does it look like?" If his so-called best friend wanted to get between him and his woman, then the gloves were off. Aidan should be his wingman right now, helping him get his girl back, not playing gatekeeper and stopping him from seeing her.

"You sure you want to be here? I might accidentally kick the ball into your pretty-boy face. Then how will you get girls into your bed? 'Cause it certainly won't be your charming personality."

Sawyer sprang to his feet, getting in Aidan's space. "Why don't you ask your sister?"

He barely saw the motion coming, and dodged to the left, but it was too late. Aidan's fist clipped him on the jaw. Sharp stabs of pain radiated through his face and his eyes watered momentarily before he blinked them clear and lunged toward the attack instead of away. His shoulder crashed into Aidan's ribs and together they went down hard on the artificial turf. He grunted when a shot connected with his kidney.

From somewhere in the distance, voices yelled at them to stop or cheered at them to hit harder—he couldn't tell. The only thing he could focus on was Aidan's face, and taking out his frustration.

He threw a fist and felt it collide with bone, but without the crunch of breaking. As another hit slammed into the side of his head, making his ear ring loudly, arms pulled on his shoulders, separating him from his target. Breaking free, he scrambled to get in another shot.

"Why did you do it? Why did you have to screw with her?" Aidan asked as he came at him again, a whirlwind of blows landing along his ribs.

"She wanted me as much as I wanted her. Deal with it."

"You think you can use her like some chick from the bar and I'm going to *deal* with it?"

"I didn't use her and I would never think of her that

way."

"Like hell you didn't." His friend pulled his fist back, ready to pulverize him again. "Then why, you son of a bitch? Why couldn't you stay away from her?"

"Because I fucking love her, okay?" Sawyer shot back, bracing for the punch, but as soon as the admission left his lips, his body went weak.

Aidan was pulled off him and a second later Sawyer was dragged to his feet. He had no strength left to fight back. Confusion flashed across Aidan's eyes.

"Enough!" shouted Jason, coming between them. "If you have issues with each other, take them off the field."

Sawyer pulled free and tugged his shirt back into place. He focused on his team captain, unable to look Aidan in the eye. "It's over. Let's get this game started."

"You're out of the game. Both of you. I can't let you take this shit out on the other team."

Sawyer sat on the bench with his head in his hands. What the hell had gotten into him? Years he'd been friends with Aidan, through girlfriend indiscretions, drunken mischief that almost got them expelled from college, and even a frat prank that could've landed them in jail, and never once had they ever gotten into a fist fight with each other. None of that had ever meant as much to him as losing Olivia.

Fuck. I love her.

But did he love the idea of a baby, too?

Aidan flopped down onto the bench beside him, wincing. "Goddamn it. I'm too old for this shit."

Sawyer laughed, his anger long gone, replaced by a mixture of regret and rejection. And pain. He wasn't bleeding anywhere he could see, but he'd definitely be bruised.

Hopefully they'd all fade before the big birthday party in a couple of weeks. The last thing he needed to do was show up there not only alone, but beat to a pulp as well.

"When did you get so good with your right hook?" he asked, rubbing a particularly tender spot along his jaw.

"I don't know. When did you fall in love with my sister?"

"Fucked if I know." He rolled his shoulders, cringing. What would he give for one of her massages now? "Listen, I didn't mean to. It just sort of…happened. And I didn't mean to sleep with her either. That just sort of happened, too."

"Oh yeah? You were walking along one day and slipped and found your dick somewhere it shouldn't be?"

"Something like that." He laughed. If he could go back to that first night with her, he'd never leave the hotel room. "How is she?"

Aidan sighed. "She's a mess, thanks to you. I've never seen her like this before, even after everything that happened with Sam. This time is different. Worse. If you really love her, then you need to figure out a way to make this better."

"How can I? She won't return my calls. Has she listened to any of my voicemails? Read the multiple emails I've sent? Texts? Anything?"

"Not as far as I know."

"Then there's not a lot I can do. I promise I'll make this right if she gives me the chance. Get her to listen to my messages, okay?" He hated begging, but when it came to Olivia, he was willing to do whatever it took.

"I'll see what I can do, but she's pretty stubborn." Aidan dabbed at the blood trickling down his chin from his busted lip. "I better go put some ice on this. I have a big meeting tomorrow and I'll have a hard time explaining why I look like I got in a bar brawl."

"Sorry. I mean it. For everything."

Aidan sighed, looking defeated. "If she decides to take you back, I'll cease and desist on the ass kicking I owe you. But you better spend the rest of your life making her happy. *If* you're lucky enough to get the chance."

"Deal."

He couldn't let Olivia walk away without ever talking to her again. What would he do without her in his life? What would happen with the baby?

These last few months had started out as a scam, but somewhere along the way, he'd gotten used to having her by his side. Now that she wasn't anymore, his whole world had shifted and he didn't see any way to get it back on track without her. Before, he couldn't imagine a future with anyone, ever. Now, he couldn't imagine a future without Olivia.

Chapter Twenty

Olivia glanced up at the sound of the key in the front door. Aidan was at a soccer game and not supposed to be home for another hour—exactly the reason she'd put on a chick flick while she had enough time to wallow alone in cheesy love story goodness.

He walked into the apartment and casually tossed his keys onto the table, as if his face weren't swollen and bruised. Springing from the couch, she went to his side.

"Are you okay?"

"Peachy." Retrieving a bag of peas from the freezer, he pressed it to his cheekbone.

"Seriously, if you don't tell me what happened, I'm going to add another bruise to your collection. Do I need to call the police?"

She sat on the couch beside Aidan while the hero from the movie declared his undying love for the heroine, and how he'd been completely devoted to her for years even when she didn't reciprocate.

Yeah, right. Like that shit would ever happen in real life.

Blinking back a fresh wave of tears, she clicked off the TV and tossed the remote.

"You don't need to call the police and I'm not interested in rehashing the story."

"Too bad. Spill it or I make you bleed again."

"I'd like to see you try," he grumbled.

She poked him in the side, playfully, but his faced scrunched up. "Oh, shit. Sorry." Guilt instantly flooded her, followed by a hearty dose of anger at whoever had done this to him. "Did you even make it to your game?"

"I made it onto the field and then was promptly sent home."

"What? Why?"

"Seems fighting is prohibited in soccer. Shame too, since I'm pretty sure I was winning."

She laughed. "What did the other player do to make you fight him?"

"Why don't you call and ask him yourself?" Aidan groaned as he rolled up to his feet, heading toward the bedroom.

Suspicion itched at the back of her brain as she followed him. "Who did you fight?"

"Sawyer."

She sucked in a quick breath. If this was how bad her brother looked and he claimed he was winning, how bad did Sawyer look?

It doesn't matter. He deserved it.

"Why?"

"Why do you think?" He sank into his bed and pulled the covers up.

"This wasn't your fight." She folded her arms across her chest.

"Someone had to defend your honor."

"My honor didn't need defending," she said, her annoyance at the situation in general peaking.

"If that's how you really feel, then why haven't you listened to his messages or returned his calls?"

She stepped back into the hallway, distancing herself. "That's none of your business."

He raised his head and peered at her with one eye slightly smaller than the other because of the swelling. A dark bruise had already formed on his cheekbone. "Apparently it is."

She started to close the door.

"Olivia," her brother called, stopping her.

"What do you need?" It annoyed her that he had taken it upon himself to fight her battle, but she didn't want to see him hurting either. "More ice? A pain killer?"

"I need you to listen to his messages. I've never seen him like this before. He's a mess. Because of you. Because of how he feels about you." He cringed as he adjusted his position on the bed. "I would love nothing more than to pummel him again for the fact that he hurt you, but you're hurting him, too. Just listen to what he has to say, then decide what you want."

He flopped back and she closed the door, ending their conversation. She didn't want to talk to him about it anymore. Not when he blamed his actions on her.

It wasn't her fault two meatheads got in a fight, and it certainly wasn't her fault that Sawyer was hurting. If he'd talked to her about the baby, about their relationship—fake relationship—and about the travel, none of this would have happened.

Pushing the guilt aside, she made up the couch and flipped off all the lights except the one on the end table. Grabbing her phone, she flipped from one website to another, randomly reading half an article then getting bored and reading something else. Against her better judgment, she clicked on her text messages, ignoring all of the previous ones from Sawyer. She wasn't ready to read them. Instead she typed the one thing she couldn't get off her mind:

Are you okay?

She nibbled her bottom lip, waiting for his reply. Thoughts raced through her mind. Was Sawyer hurt badly? Did he get home okay? Did he have to go to the hospital? A moment later her phone vibrated.

I'll survive the bruises. My broken heart's another story.

Yeah, right.

She wrote back quickly, hitting send before she thought it through. Getting into it with him was not her intension, now or ever. She'd simply wanted to make sure he wasn't lying in a hospital room on her account.

If you cared enough to check on me, then care enough to listen to the voicemails I left you. Please.

She didn't reply. Typing a response involved knowing what she wanted, which she had, an hour ago. She wasn't so sure anymore. Seeing his name on the screen made her chest feel as if *she'd* been someone's punching bag. Her heart ached with longing for him.

Still there?

Should she answer him or pretend she'd walked away from her phone, gone to sleep, anything?

A moment later, a new text came through.

There's so much I need to say. So much you need to hear.

I gotta go.

She typed frantically as her vision blurred. Whatever he wanted to say, whatever he wanted her to hear, she wasn't playing along. Couldn't. Her heart was already broken by his rejection. Nothing he said now would heal it.

Wait.

Bye Sawyer.

Olivia clutched her phone to her chest as tears streamed down her cheeks. Why had she initiated the conversation with him? What good would it do? Their agreement was over, null and void. He wouldn't get the cabin, and she would never get a job reference. Basically they'd wasted two months of their lives for nothing but a couple romps in the sack and a whole lot of heartache.

And a baby.

But even as she thought it, she corrected herself. There was so much more to Sawyer than a good time in bed, although sex with him had been beyond fantastic. That wasn't what she missed most, though. It was the late night TV and popcorn on the couch. Shared conversation on the commute to and from work. Laughing with his family while cuddling together in front of the campfire. Those were the things she'd long for.

Her phone vibrated again, and she hesitated before flipping it over to read the message. It was simple—words she needed to hear but never thought she would. And yet, not at all the words she wanted to hear.

I'm sorry.

Forcing a hitched breath into her lungs, she went to voicemail. If he could apologize, then she could listen. Forty-seven messages waited for her. The man was nothing if not persistent.

By message three, she knew one thing to be true—she'd grossly overreacted to the announcement that he had to travel. He'd done nothing wrong. This wasn't his suggestion or his choice. He didn't want to leave her and the baby behind. Marcus had made it a condition to the agreement. But that didn't change the fact he was leaving her. She didn't want a boyfriend, real or fake, who would come and go as the wind blew him. She wanted someone by her side, always. Maybe this trip for Marcus was temporary, but so was a future together, since nothing in his numerous voicemails led her to believe he'd changed his mind on the idea of commitment or bachelorhood.

Sawyer still wanted right now. She still wanted forever. Even if she'd never get the forever she wanted, after listening to his voice she knew she had to try to get him the forever *he* wanted. And she knew exactly what to do.

. . .

Sawyer hated the antiseptic smell of the hospital, but holding the tiny, warm, eight-pound bundle of sweetness in his arms definitely helped to make the place less terrifying. He wasn't a baby kind of guy, but this one didn't completely send him running for the hills either. Maybe it was because the child was his niece. His family. Or maybe it was because she was only a few hours old and couldn't do anything but open her eyes for a few seconds at a time and make the world's softest cooing noises. How could anyone not like that?

Surely it had nothing to do with him becoming a pathetic, heartbroken ball of mush since he'd fallen in love with Olivia and subsequently lost her forever. It absolutely had nothing to do with the fact that there was a little mound of sweetness growing inside of Olivia either. One he'd helped create.

The pain of his bruised face had almost completely disappeared the second he'd seen her name pop up on his phone after his fight with Aidan. He'd even convinced himself she would listen to his messages and come running back to him, but it had been a week and nothing. No more texts. Not a single call. Nada.

"Where's Olivia?" Gran asked.

Should he tell them the truth or hold off a little longer and pray she came back to him before the birthday party next week?

"She woke up with a scratchy throat and didn't want to risk passing anything on to the baby," he said. It was the first excuse he could think of that would be accepted without hesitation. "She'll come by and see Misha as soon as she's feeling better."

The baby opened her mouth in a big yawn then smacked her lips together, wiggling in his arms. "She's doing something. I don't know what. Want her back?" he asked. He was comfortable holding the baby for a few minutes, but if she needed anything besides a comfy arm to curl up in, then she needed her mom.

"Hopefully Olivia will be feeling better in time for the party," Gran said.

That could be a viable excuse if needed.

"I hope so too. I know she's been looking forward to another weekend at the cabin."

"I'm sure she is," Tyler said, a note of distaste in his voice.

The two men eyed each other, but neither spoke the secrets they were privy to. Neither could afford to be out of Gran's good graces so close to the party.

"Well, why wouldn't she? We have a fantastic time together," Gran said.

"I gotta run." His voice fell as he said the words, hating himself for lying, not once, but multiple times. "I've got to get back to work. I'll stop in and see Misha again soon. Make sure you get some rest, Sophia."

Before waiting for a reply, he bent and gave the baby a quick kiss on the head then walked out the door.

Gran and Gramps wanted to leave the cabin to someone worthy, and there was a time, not that long ago, when he would have said he was that person. Could he still say that now? He'd swindled his way into Olivia's life, making her an offer she couldn't refuse, all so he could benefit. Then he lied to his family about his relationship. They had opened their hearts and their home to her, all because he'd told them she was his. But she wasn't his, never had been.

This latest deceit felt even worse. Instead of coming clean, he'd lied again, faked her illness, and was even planning on using it for the party so he'd still have a chance to make the cabin his.

They wanted to leave the cabin to someone who would have a family someday. Now he was faced with that very real future and he had no idea if he even wanted it. Did he want a future with Olivia and the baby?

He was a poor excuse for a grandson and an even worse human being.

He had to tell his grandparents the truth. It didn't matter if they gave him the cabin anymore. The only thing that mattered was making things right with Olivia. Maybe if he admitted the truth about his feelings for her to himself, to her, and to his family, he'd be able to salvage their relationship before he lost her and the baby forever.

Chapter Twenty-One

Sawyer slumped in a deck chair and downed his first shot. There'd be many more of these before the party was over, but it was early and he needed to pace himself. Being a slobbering drunk wasn't an option. As much as he wanted to let the alcohol numb his pain, he had to face this moment head on, sober.

Another week had gone by and Olivia still hadn't contacted him. Obviously his heartfelt apologies on her voicemail weren't enough. Aidan hadn't spoke to him since their fight on the field either. He'd called them both, multiple times, but hadn't gotten through to either of them. Seemed Olivia wasn't ready to forgive him and his friend was following her lead.

He'd even shown up at the apartment but wasn't allowed up. Waiting outside during times when he thought they'd be coming or going hadn't done any good either. Somehow they always managed to elude him.

In one half-baked scheme, he'd destroyed a lifelong

friendship, was about to alienate himself from his family, and managed to lose the only woman he'd ever loved.

Bravo. Brav-fucking-o.

"You look in good spirits today," Tyler said, before bursting into deep belly laughter. "I can't even say that with a straight face. She's gone, isn't she? Left you high and dry when you needed her the most."

"I don't know what you're talking about." He planned on telling the truth but the thought that Tyler would get to hear it first disgusted him. "Why don't you be a good father and go cuddle your baby."

"I did that already. In front of Gran. Besides, Misha is eating and I can't exactly help with that part."

The end was near and there wasn't a damn thing he could do about it. He'd have to suck it up and let go. He'd still have the memories of his family, with or without the cabin. Besides that, after bringing Olivia here, he wasn't sure he could picture himself at the cabin without her. Every time he thought about coming here in the future, she infiltrated his thoughts. And not only her—the baby, too, a tiny Sawyer-Olivia hybrid, toddling around on the beach, splashing in the waves, sleeping in the back bedroom that he would convert into a nursery. Coming here now would remind him of everything he'd lost.

"Enjoy it, man. I hope the money helps you out with Misha."

Tyler's smile wavered. "You're giving up?"

Sawyer shrugged. "I'm done. You win. Embrace it." He grabbed a beer and left Tyler stunned.

"If everyone could gather around please," spoke someone into the microphone. "Grandma and Grandpa Sterling would like to make an announcement before we cut the cake."

Instantly his palms grew sweaty. He'd hoped to speak to them privately before they dealt with the cabin, but it appeared he'd lost his opportunity. Maybe it was better this way. Then everyone could hear his story firsthand instead of it filtering through the usual gossip chains, morphing into something different along the way.

Gran and Gramps took their seats at the head table. Their smiles calmed him momentarily before he remembered he would be the one who ruined their day. As they were being handed the microphone, he stepped forward, intent on saying his piece and telling the truth before they made their final decision.

Fair would be spilling Tyler's secret to sell the cabin at the same time, but it wasn't Sawyer's place to say anything. And the sooner he stopped caring about the cabin the better, no matter how much it hurt to let his home go.

"Before you make your announcement, there's something I need to say." He stepped through the crowd. His grandparents turned to him, surprise on their faces.

"Whatever it is, I'm sure it can wait," Tyler said, glaring at him.

"Relax. This has nothing to do with you. This is all about what I've done."

"What do you mean, dear?" Gran asked, sitting forward in her chair.

"It's about Olivia and me, and our relationship." He paused unsure of how to say exactly what he needed to.

"Where is she? I haven't seen her yet today. Is she still ill?"

"I'm here, Gran," Olivia said, rushing up to the head

table, her arms wide for a hug. "I'm so sorry I'm late. Traffic was terrible, and then I got lost. Really, I couldn't be more embarrassed. I brought you these." She thrust a bouquet of calla lilies and orchids at them.

"Thank you, dear. You're just in time. Sawyer was about to tell us something important. About you and him. Sounds exciting." Her eyes twinkled with excitement.

"He was? Oh, um, well, yes. Perhaps he should do that another time." She stared at him as if trying to turn him to stone, but he wouldn't be silenced.

In fact, the sight of her recharged him, surging him with energy and confidence. He'd waited weeks for a chance to tell her how he felt, and now he could. And she'd have to listen to him here.

"What I have to say needs to happen now."

"Really, sweetheart, let's not bore your family with our…issues." She twisted her hands together as if they were the source of her discomfort. Sadly, he was the one who got that honor.

"Olivia and I aren't really dating."

She gasped, as did a few other people. Gran, however, looked calm as ever.

"Sawyer, really. Now isn't the time!" Olivia's voice had an edge of nervousness to it, but there was something else behind it too, almost as if she were holding back her emotions and nearly failing. The glistening in her eyes told him he was probably right.

"No. Now. When I found out you wanted to leave the deed for the cabin to one of us, I was thrilled. I've loved the cabin since I was a child. It's where so many of my memories of my parents are. It's the only place I really feel close to them, and it's been the only home I've known since their accident."

"We know, dear."

"But then you said you only wanted to leave it to someone who would pass it down to their children and my hopes crumbled. Why on earth would you ever leave the cabin to a bachelor like me when your other choice is Tyler, Sophia, and Misha? I knew I was sunk. I couldn't compete."

He paused, taking a deep breath.

"No," Olivia whispered, moving toward him, but Gran's hand on her arm froze her in place.

"And then I realized I could compete if I had a relationship that might lead to something more in the future. At least, it had to look like I had a relationship. So I made Olivia an offer she couldn't refuse.

"We were pretty convincing too. It was fun, in a way, playing the part of the loving boyfriend, bringing my girl around to family dinner so I wasn't the only single one for a change. It felt nice. Comforting. And then it was more than that, and before I knew it, I'd fallen for her. This girl, who was only supposed to be my temporary girlfriend until after this party, wormed her way into my heart and took root there."

The ache that had been in his chest for weeks dissipated slightly, evaporating like fog in sunshine. This was right. Telling everyone what he'd done and how he honestly felt was the thing he should have done all along.

"I know telling you this will cost me the cabin. I'll miss the summer weekends here, the moon reflecting off the lake on a clear night, the smell of campfires, but it's okay, because it's only a place. And it's a place that will never be the same, because now whenever I think of the cabin, I imagine Olivia there with me. But she won't be. I screwed up."

Tears pooled in his eyes, but he didn't bother to try and blink them away. What was the use? There would only be more to follow. May as well give in, finally. He'd spilled his heart and soul for everyone to see, what were a few tears in the mix?

• • •

Was this really happening? Had she walked into an episode of some alternate reality television show?

"What the hell are you doing?" she asked in a whispered yell as she went to Sawyer's side. "Are you out of your mind? You've blown any chance you had at scoring the cabin."

"It doesn't matter anymore."

"So this last three months was a waste? It was all for nothing?"

"I wouldn't say that."

"What the hell would you say then? I'm out of a job and an apartment and now you won't even get the cabin. Sounds like a win to me!" She scolded him, barely controlling her voice so the others around them couldn't hear.

"Are you finished yet, Sawyer?" Gran asked.

He shrugged. "For now. I'm sorry I interrupted your announcement."

"Quite alright. I'm glad you've got that off your chest. I'm sure it's been bothering you for some time."

Olivia hugged herself, ready for the scolding.

"As you all know, we came here to celebrate our birthdays as well as to gift the deed to the family cabin. I'm sure interest is piqued after Sawyer's heartfelt confession. So without further ado, we'll get on with it. When we decided to do this, we hoped to leave the place to someone who would one day pass it down through the family. And while we still hope that is the case, we have realized the person who takes over for us has to love it as much as we do. Sawyer, the cabin is yours."

"Are you kidding me, Gran? Seriously, Gramps? He lied, and you're giving him the cabin as a reward?" Tyler stopped short of stomping his foot but otherwise threw a temper tantrum.

"Sawyer might have lied, but his hopes for a future at the cabin were honest, which is more than I can say for the grandson who was only looking to make a few bucks," Gramps said, speaking up for the first time.

"I don't know what you're talking about." Tyler turned a brilliant shade of crimson.

"Oh? I'm sure your real estate agent would be interested to hear that, since she's already spending the commission she planned to earn next spring. Seems she's got quite the mouth on her, and never shuts it. Told the whole bloody town about the upcoming listing, just in case anyone knew of a buyer. Smart cookie, that one."

Olivia laughed at Gramps' sarcasm.

"Are you really giving me the cabin?" Sawyer asked. "After everything I told you? Aren't you upset?"

"Heavens no. We knew something was fishy right from the start and had you two figured out long ago."

"Why didn't you say anything?" he asked, his voice filled with disbelief and curiosity.

"What fun would there be in that?" Gran laughed.

"She added a nice bit of eye candy, I think they say, to our family dinners. And I like that she kept you on your toes. I wasn't ready to see her leave," Gramps added.

Her cheeks burned. She'd never been called eye candy by an eighty-year-old man before.

"Oh stop," Gran said, swatting at Gramps. "We had the deed made up shortly after we figured you out. We knew that if you, the king of bachelors, were willing to even pretend to have a girlfriend to get the cabin, that it must be pretty special to you. Later, when we found out about the soon-to-be listing in the area, we knew we'd made the right choice."

"You could have told us sooner and saved us all the heartache," Tyler said, whining.

He didn't even understand the meaning of the word. Heartache had nothing to do with losing a possession like the cabin. Real heartache came from losing the only person who mattered in your world, losing the only man you ever loved.

Back when Sam had left her, practically at the altar, she'd thought he was the love of her life. But now, knowing Sawyer, being with him this entire time, seeing what he would sacrifice to tell the truth about their relationship, she knew what real, whole-hearted love was. What she'd felt for Sam all those years ago was like puppy love, a crush. What she felt for Sawyer was all encompassing, can't-deny-it, chick flick style love.

"And spoil the big announcement today?" Gran said. "No. We wanted to wait and see how this all played out. Not exactly how we hoped, I'm afraid."

Gran's gaze fell to Olivia.

She swallowed around the lump of emotion in her

throat. She'd barely kept it together this long. No way could she hold it in under Gran's watchful gaze.

"Congratulations. I'm really happy for you, but I have to go." She spun on her heel to walk away, but he grabbed her arm, stopping her.

"No. I'm not letting you run away again. Not until you hear what I have to say."

"I've heard it all. I listened to your voicemails. I know how you feel. Or at least how you feel right now."

"You listened to them and still didn't contact me? Why?"

"Because it doesn't change the fact that we want different things in life. I want stability. Roots. A place to call my own and someone to share it with me. Someone who plans to stick around forever, not just for now."

She bit her lower lip hard, trying desperately to stave off the sadness threatening to cripple her if she gave into it. She'd been strong this long; she could be strong a little longer.

"What if I told you I wanted forever, too?" Sawyer asked.

Chapter Twenty-Two

"Don't, Sawyer. Don't do this to me," Olivia said, her voice on the edge of breaking.

Sliding his hand down her arm, he took her hand in his, gripping it tightly so she wouldn't slip away. He couldn't live through that again. He hoped she saw the truth of his feelings in his eyes, heard it in his words. "I mean it. The day you walked into my apartment was the day my life changed. The day you walked out of my office and didn't look back was the day my world ended."

She sucked in a hitched breath and he wanted more than anything to pull her into his arms and kiss her. But he wouldn't. Not yet.

"I didn't realize the mess I'd made of my life until you showed me how good really living could be. Right from the start, you cared about me, my life, my future, and not because you had to as part of the deal, but because you wanted to."

"I shouldn't have tried to change you. You're perfect the

way you are," she said softly.

"You did change me. For the better."

Sawyer looked around at all the people watching their moment and knew his time was running out. Taking a deep breath, he geared up for his final push, the one that would hopefully land him the ultimate prize—Olivia.

"The day you left, I'd planned on taking you out and asking you to be my girlfriend for real. I wasn't sure what the future would bring, but I knew I wanted you in it. I had a position made for you at Sterling. A permanent one. It's still there if you want it. I wasn't sure how I'd sort out the whole traveling thing with work, but I knew I'd do whatever it took to find a way to keep you and get that deal, too. I'd fly back and forth across the ocean every other weekend if I had to."

"You don't have to change who you are for me, and you don't have to sign on for a future you don't really want. The baby and I will be fine on our own."

"What's that about a baby?" Gran asked, sitting forward in her seat.

Olivia placed her hand on her stomach. "I'm pregnant."

"That's wonderful, dear!" Gran cheered.

"And I'll raise the baby on my own. All I ever wanted was someone to share my life with, have a family with, and now I have the family even if I don't have the husband to go along with it."

"There's no doubt in my mind you would do a damn good job as a single mother," said Sawyer, "but that's not what I want for you or for our child. Who I am now and what I want in the future are different because of having you in my life, and I'm okay with that. Fuck, I'm great with that."

"Language, son," Gramps piped up.

"Shush up," Gran said, swatting him.

"Olivia, I love you. I'll love you today and tomorrow and forever if you'll let me. I'll give up the Marcus project if that's what it takes to win you back. You are more important to me than any other person in this whole world."

Tears flowed freely down her cheeks and he hoped with every fiber in his being that they were tears of happiness, because if they weren't, he'd made a huge ass of himself in front of his entire family for nothing.

"I love you, too, Sawyer," she whispered.

"What did you say, dear? We're eighty. You're gonna have to speak louder than that. Someone get her the mic." Gramps waved at the nearest person.

Olivia laughed then spoke louder. "I love him too."

The grin spreading across Sawyer's face was so wide and proud that it almost hurt. She loved him, and he couldn't be happier. Well, he could be.

He dropped to his knee, not letting go of her hand. "I don't have a ring."

"Sawyer, come here!" Gran called.

"Not now, Gran. I'm kind in the middle of something," he called back, rolling his eyes but trying not to break the magic of the moment. "And I know this is unexpected since we literally just made up. But—"

"Come here, Sawyer. Come." Gran waved her arms like she was signaling a 747 into a coat closet.

"Are you for real? No, Gran. Please stop interrupting me. As I was saying, I would be so honored if you would agree to spend forever with me...and my apparently crazy-assed family."

"Language. And for God's sake, get your ass over here

before your grandmother has a heart attack." Gramps smacked his hand on the tabletop.

Sawyer shook his head. "He only does that when he really means business. I better go."

Olivia looked as if she was about to faint. The way this impromptu proposal was going so far, that probably wasn't far from reality. He rose and strode impatiently to his meddling and completely annoying grandparents.

"What?" he asked through gritted teeth.

Gran spun the ring on her finger until it finally came off. It wasn't the biggest diamond in the world, but it was beautiful. "Use my ring. A woman needs a ring when she's getting proposed to. It's not quite the same without one."

"Really?"

"It's done us well for the last million years or so of marriage. I'm sure it can see you through until you find one she likes better, unless she'd like to keep this one. It has to go to someone eventually. I'm kind of looking forward to seeing it on a new, younger finger."

"Thank you, Gran."

"Now hurry up. The poor girl is standing there all alone."

He strode back over to Olivia and resumed his position on bended knee. "Would you do me the great honor of agreeing to spend the rest of forever with me? I promise to love you, to be the best father I can be, and to stop being an ignorant jerk who can't see a good thing when it's right in front of him." He held out Gran's ring, his breath trapped in his throat by a paralyzing fear that, after all of this, she might say no.

She slipped her finger into the ring. "I will totally marry you!"

Since the moment she'd walked out of his life and he'd realized he'd fallen in love—and not any kind of love, but full-blown, can't-live-without-her, cry-at-country-songs-on-the-radio kind of love—he'd been dreaming about kissing her even one more time. To know he'd get to do it for a lifetime was almost too good to be true.

Pressing his lips to hers, kissing her deeply, thoroughly, it was as if the rest of the world was put on hold. Nothing else mattered or even existed. Nothing else would ever matter as much to him as this woman and the child she nurtured inside.

When he'd finally had enough of her to last him a few minutes, he pulled back. The band started playing, people were clapping and shouting, but nothing could distract him from the woman in front of him, the woman he loved. Together they swayed gently to the music, as others joined in around them. Still, he never took his eyes off of her. "You are the most gorgeous thing I have ever seen. I must be the luckiest man in the world."

"You're not so bad yourself," she said, when he finally stopped kissing her long enough that she could talk. "I still can't believe I snagged the bachelor. People were surprised to hear you had a girlfriend. What will they say when they find out you went and got yourself a fiancée?"

"I don't give a damn what they think, but you might. The women will probably hate you for taking me off the market." He hoped she heard the teasing in his voice.

"Think pretty highly of yourself, don't you?"

He laughed, spinning her out then pulling her tight to his body again. "Now that I have you back, and you're all mine, forever, I plan on taking you to my bed and keeping you there." He grinned wickedly.

"Then I better stock up on refreshments and snacks because my appetite came back with a vengeance," she said, moving as if she were about to go in search of those items, but he held her close.

"Nope. I'm not letting you out of my sight for at least the next seven months or so. Sorry, you're stuck with me."

"Isn't that going to be kind of hard when you're on one side of the ocean and I'm on the other?" He could see in her eyes she didn't really want to bring up the subject, but the issue needed to be addressed.

"I had a thought about that," he said.

"Oh?" she asked, her curiosity obviously piqued.

"You're a world traveler, so you know how to find your way around new countries. I think the best way for you to help Sterling Enterprises—if you accept the job I've created for you—is for you to come with me. See the world with me for the next few months."

"Really? What will Marcus say about that?"

"I'm sure he'll agree, since it was your ideas that won him over to begin with. What do you say?"

"What about the baby?" Her hand pressed to her belly.

"There are doctors in other countries, and I'll make Marcus pay for the best ones. And we'll have you back before your third trimester."

"As much as I look forward to putting down roots and settling in here, it was nice to wake up to a new sunrise every few weeks when I was backpacking."

"Is that a yes?"

She nodded. "Yes! I'd love to. I can't wait to see the sights with you. When we're not working, of course."

"And when we're not busy in between the sheets, of course. I can't wait to do you on every continent."

"Stop." She giggled and pushed him away playfully.

"That's not what you'll be saying later."

"You're such a romantic."

"Admit it, you love it, and you can't wait to do me, too."

"I admit nothing."

She melted in his arms when he kissed her, her hands roaming his body in a way that was almost inappropriate at his grandparents' birthday party, and he loved every second of her touch. Just when he thought he had his life all figured out, Olivia came into it and turned it upside down. And thank God she had because he couldn't imagine his world any other way.

Epilogue

"Where are you taking me?" Olivia asked Sawyer, as the ground beneath her feet shuddered.

The night had started out romantic—a formal dinner on a terrace overlooking Paris, delicious food, soft music—she couldn't have asked for more. Then he'd insisted she put on this ridiculous blindfold and had carted her off to some mystery location.

She was all for a good surprise, but this pushed her patience a little too far.

"We're almost there," he said, his breath warm on her earlobe, tickling her.

"Where exactly? The ground moved. Last time I checked, it wasn't supposed to do that." She shrieked as her world shook again, and clung to his arm so hard she was probably leaving bruises. Good—he deserved them after this.

"One more minute, sugar."

The endearment still sent a tingle up her spine, even

after the months of use. She'd never get used to how good it felt to be with him, be loved by him.

As he led her forward to what she hoped was their final destination, wind whipped through her hair and up her skirt. Thank goodness her hair was tied back and her dress was long and form fitting, hugging her growing belly, or she'd be a real sight. Suddenly, her blindfold was removed and Sawyer stood in front of her, staring at her with eyes she knew she'd never get tired of peering into. Breaking his gaze, she looked around and realized he'd taken her to the top of the Eiffel Tower. Millions of twinkling lights cast an amber glow around them, like giant fireflies.

"What's going on?" she asked.

"These last couple of months—traveling with you, working with you, being inside you in multiple countries—have been the best months of my life." He winked and she held herself back from hitting him. Only he would mix a heartfelt moment with sex talk, and she loved him for it.

Absolutely, unequivocally, whole-heartedly, she loved him with her entire being.

"Traveling on my own after college was the trip of a lifetime, but traveling with you is even better. Everyday I'm so thankful to be here with you."

Tears threatened to well up in her eyes. So many things could have kept them apart, and yet, somehow they'd managed to find a way to each other.

"I know we said we'd wait until we got back to the States to get married, and I never even thought I'd be a marrying kind of guy, but I am now, because of you. I don't want to wait any longer to make it official."

He stepped aside, clearing her view. A minister stood

waiting for them under the arch of the tower, and on his signal a quartet began playing. She didn't recognize the song, but it didn't matter. Slow and liquid, it called to her, urging her down the makeshift aisle.

"I know I already asked you this once, but tonight I mean right now. Will you marry me?"

Olivia bit her lip, trying desperately to hold back her emotions before they overflowed in a very snot-filled, least-beautiful-wedding-photo-ever type way. "What about our families? What about Gran and Gramps? Won't they be upset if they don't get to see us get married?"

He grinned. "Probably. That's why we shouldn't tell them."

"What do you mean? How can we explain the fact we aren't having a wedding back home anymore?"

"Simple. We'll still have a wedding, a reception, all of it. It will be a real wedding in every way, except one—you'll already be mine and I'll already be yours."

"Another scam, huh? You really think that's the best way to start our marriage together?" she asked, already feeling excited.

"It sort of works for us. What do you say? Marry me tonight. Love me forever?"

He loved her enough that he wanted to marry her early, privately, right this second. How could she refuse the desire of the man who was her whole world?

"Let the hoax begin. And if Gran figures us out this time, we're doomed."

"But at least we'll be doomed together."

Acknowledgments

I'd like to say a huge thank you to my agent Jill Marsal of Marsal Lyon Literary Agency. Without your continued guidance and support I'd probably be stuck in a plot hole somewhere. Your time and effort is always appreciated!

I'd also like to give a big shout out to my awesome editor at Entangled Publishing, Alethea Spiridon Hopson. Your editing notes are thoughtful, insightful, and always set me on the right path. Thank you so much for helping me to make my stories as good as they can be.

About the Author

Heather Thurmeier is a lover of strawberry margaritas, a hater of spiders, and a reality TV junkie. Born and raised in the Canadian prairies, she now lives in New York with her husband and kids where she's become some kind of odd Canuck-Yankee hybrid. When she's not busy taking care of the kids and pets, Heather's writing her next romance, which will probably be filled with sassy heroines, sexy heroes who will make your heart pound, laugh out loud moments, and always a happily ever after. She loves to hear from readers on social media and her website!

Also by Heather Thurmeier...

THE WEDDING HOAX

Wedding gown designer Daisy Willows is desperate for an influx of cash to cover her mother's homecare bills. With subscriptions to his father's wedding magazine plummeting, playboy Cole Benton needs to find a way to stimulate sales, and *fast*. But then a renowned bridal show expo owner offers to bail them out—*if* they rekindle their failed relationship and plan the fake wedding of the century. Except, with all the ring shopping and kissing upon request, they're having a hard time remembering that their big white wedding is a big white *lie*...